OUR TOWN

and the

COSMIC ONE-ACTS

Books by Thornton Wilder

Novels

The Cabala

The Bridge of San Luis Rey

The Woman of Andros

Heaven's My Destination

The Ides of March

The Eighth Day

Theophilus North

Collections of Short Plays

The Angel that Troubled the Waters

The Long Christmas Dinner & Other Plays in One Act

The Collected Short Plays of Thornton Wilder Vol. 1

The Collected Short Plays of Thornton Wilder Vol. 2

Plays

Our Town

The Merchant of Yonkers

The Skin of Our Teeth

The Matchmaker

The Alcestiad

The Beaux' Stratagem (with Ken Ludwig)

A Doll's House

Nonfiction

American Characteristics & Other Essays

The Journals of Thornton Wilder, 1939–1961

The Selected Letters of Thornton Wilder

The Letters of Gertrude Stein and Thornton Wilder

A Tour of the Darkling Plain: The Finnegans Wake Letters of Thornton Wilder and Adaline Glasheen

OUR TOWN

and the

COSMIC ONE-ACTS

The Long Christmas Dinner,

The Happy Journey to Trenton and Camden,

and *Pullman Car Hiawatha*

THORNTON WILDER

HARPERPERENNIAL  MODERNCLASSICS

NEW YORK • LONDON • TORONTO • SYDNEY • NEW DELHI • AUCKLAND

HARPERPERENNIAL MODERNCLASSICS

HarperCollins books may be purchased for educational, business, or sales promotional use. For information, please email the Special Markets Department at SPsales@harpercollins.com.

FIRST HARPER PERENNIAL MODERN CLASSICS EDITION PUBLISHED 2025.

Library of Congress Cataloging-in-Publication Data has been applied for.

ISBN 978-0-06-346562-6 (pbk.)

26 27 28 29 30 LBC 6 5 4 3 2

Contents

Foreword

In 1931, Thornton Wilder finished writing a set of six short plays. Some members of his public viewed them as a departure from his "real" work: At thirty-four, Wilder was best known for his fiction, particularly *The Bridge of San Luis Rey.* The plays received modest world premieres late in the year, when student actors performed them at Yale University, Antioch College, and the University of Chicago, where Wilder was a visiting lecturer. The one-acts might have amounted to a minor episode in his long and varied career—except that three of them turned out to be masterpieces.

In *The Happy Journey to Trenton and Camden*, *Pullman Car Hiawatha*, and *The Long Christmas Dinner*, Wilder used radically freewheeling form (pantomimed props, time leaps, an all-knowing Stage Manager) to offer an insightful, deeply felt, occasionally devastating depiction of human life. Even now, no American dramatist has done a more compact job of placing the minutiae of our daily routines alongside the vast mysteries of existence, asking us to consider the relationship between them. (Wilder himself was the first to label them "cosmic.")

Playwrights, it goes without saying, like to see their plays produced. But Wilder was just as happy to see these one-acts being *read*: In a letter to his German translator, he said that he considered them "belles lettres." By placing the cosmic plays alongside *Our Town*, this volume makes it easier than ever for readers to appreciate all four, both singly and together. *Our Town* seems less like a one-time departure from the humdrum conventions of naturalism and more like the culmination of a series of daring studies and trials. The cosmic one-acts seem less like diversions from Wilder's main work and more like the earliest bloom of a singular dramatic genius—a combination of human understanding and delight in novelty that renders him, among other things, the most successful experimental playwright the country has produced.

If Wilder's cosmic plays are new to you, it's likely because American theater, as an institution, doesn't know what to do with one-acts. But among the people who explore the less-traveled byways of world drama, Wilder's little masterpieces have long been celebrated—even revered. Consider *The Long Christmas Dinner.* The historian and scholar John Gassner called it "the most beautiful one-act play in English prose"; the legendary director Tyrone Guthrie called it variously "the greatest play of our epoch" and "one of the truly great plays of the human spirit"; and Orson Welles admitted that he stole its premise—a family's history unfolding via snapshots of a recurring meal—for the breakfast-table scene in *Citizen Kane.* Wilder, ever the teacher, would have been especially pleased to see that generations of writers have drawn inspiration from his big little plays, a legacy that's beautifully described in the pages that follow by one of his most acclaimed successors: the MacArthur fellow and Pulitzer Prize–finalist Sarah Ruhl.

Jeremy McCarter
Literary Executor, Thornton Wilder Estate
2025

Introduction

Wilder and His Influence, in Four Good Cries

To write even a sentence in the same volume as the great plays of Thornton Wilder is an almost religious honor for me. His plays are holy to me. To prepare, I made a pilgrimage to Wilder's old house in Hamden, Connecticut, while I was in New Haven teaching. I walked with a friend who lives in Hamden, and we circled around Wilder's old brown house with its beautiful view of the hilltops. The house isn't outwardly fancy (though he called it "The House the *Bridge* Built," referring to his Pulitzer Prize–winning novel, *The Bridge of San Luis Rey*). It looks like a good place to hide, peer out at the trees, write, and listen to the loud chirping of insects. I picked up a miniature pinecone that had fallen on the grass and put it in my pocket.

And I thought about pinecones, and literary family trees.

My literary family tree is deeply indebted to Wilder, as is a whole generation of contemporary playwrights. Wilder writes in his preface to *Three Plays*, "I became dissatisfied with the theatre-because I was unable to lend credence to such childish attempts to be 'real.' I began writing one-act plays that tried to capture not verisimilitude but reality." With that aesthetic boldness, with that brushstroke, Wilder changed theater forever.

I am often most moved by moments in the theater that happen with no scenery, no fancy lights. Wilder writes, "Our claim, our hope, our despair are in the mind—not in things, not in 'scenery.'" Wilder's plays reach for the sublime ordinary, for in-the-moment simplicity, not lacquered with technical effects. Not only is that kind of theater accessible to everyone as "poor theater" (and also quite sustainable), but also, the aesthetic emphasis lands, as a result, squarely on the language.

I spoke to Thornton Wilder's nephew, Tappan, before writing this essay. We talked about how Thornton was an extraordinarily good listener, how he died in his sleep, how he was happy (for a writer), but lonely. We talked of Gertrude Stein, Noh drama, and the Baroque's influence on Wilder. But Tappan finally told me, when writing your introduction, speak from the heart. And so that is what I will attempt, offering you my tears.

1.

I am in midair sobbing. The flight attendant gently pats my arm and says, "Are you all right?" I nod, blow my nose, and indicate that I'm watching a movie. A snippet of *Our Town* is being performed in the film *Wonder.* At Emily's final speech, I crumple, disarmed and sideswiped. No fair. Especially in midair. What is it about crying while in midair with strangers all around?

The theater of Wilder, borrowed for even a moment in a film, somehow has the ability to stand in for theater itself and also for life itself, and make me cry about life's impermanence. Rather than writing about a contemporary issue, or a mighty conflict, Wilder wrote about the human condition—the great invisible expanses in the heart. The Stage Manager in *Our Town* says, "We all know that *something* is eternal. And it ain't houses and it ain't names, and it ain't earth, and it ain't even the stars . . . everybody knows in their bones that *something* is eternal, and that something has to do with human beings."

Emily's goodbye to the world, imbued with her newfound consciousness of life passing *as it is lived*, never fails to move me. A gift to an actress, the speech is also a gift to every audience member who witnesses the play—a reminder of how to live. Emily asks, "Do any human beings ever realize life while they live it?—every, every minute?" The Stage Manager answers, "No . . . the saints and poets, maybe—they do some." One surmises that Wilder was just such a poet—that he realized life as he lived it, at least some, at least enough to write it all down.

2.

I am twenty-four, sobbing on a Bonanza bus somewhere between Providence, Rhode Island, and New York City, as I read a first draft of my teacher Paula Vogel's new play: *The Long Christmas Ride Home.*

Paula writes in her introduction, "I want us to emulate Mr. Wilder's great gift to American theatre in presentational, rather than representational, theatre." The title of the play makes her homage to Wilder's *The Long Christmas Dinner* crystal clear. *The Long Christmas Dinner* is a formal feat, a reinvention of how time can function onstage, and has influenced many contemporary playwrights, whether or not they say so. With no scenery but five chairs onstage, the architecture of Vogel's play also references *The Happy Journey to Trenton and Camden*, in which four kitchen chairs become a family in an automobile. Vogel looked to Wilder for ways to compress time, to ghost the stage, to speak directly to the audience without all that "bric-a-brac" and scenery, and to borrow Eastern aesthetics, creating a floating world onstage. In Wilder's introduction to *The Happy Journey to Trenton and Camden*, he writes, "The healthiest ages of the theatre have been marked by the fact that there was the least literally representative scenery." And so, Wilder's Stage Manager punches the "tires" of the family's invisible car and makes it clear that the journey is the destination.

There are notes in Wilder's early journals about the revelation of Japanese aesthetics, and a note written later saying he wished he'd been introduced to Japanese Noh plays earlier. Wilder explains Noh drama in this way: "An actor makes a tour of the stage and we know that he is making a long journey." I, too, love the structure of Japanese Noh plays and their focus on impermanence. Nothing could be more different from Aristotelian structure and catharsis, or from a Christian structure of moral learning and repentance. In a Noh drama, a traveler is our guide and speaks directly to the audience (not unlike the Stage Manager in *Our Town*). This traveler, or *waki*, introduces us to a principal actor who often meets a ghost, unrecognizable to them. When the actor recognizes the ghost, dances with or embraces the ghost, the play is over. Noh structure might seem opaque to many Western audiences, and yet so many playwrights have been influenced by it. I, too, borrowed Noh structure when I wrote the play *Eurydice*. Eurydice meets a ghost (her father), does not recognize the ghost, then recognizes the ghost, dances with the ghost, and the play is over shortly thereafter.

Was I thinking about Noh or was I thinking about Wilder when I wrote that play, or both? When I wrote the stage directions in which Eurydice descends to the underworld,

> *The underworld.*
> *There is no set change . . .*
> *The movement to the underworld is marked*
> *by the entrance of stones.*

I might have been thinking of Noh, or I might have been thinking of Wilder thinking of Noh. Or I might have been thinking about my teacher Paula Vogel thinking of Wilder.

3.

I am sobbing in the theater, specifically at Playwrights Horizons in New York City, watching Dan LeFranc's play *The Big Meal*. In this play, a family eats at a restaurant over a few lifespans; as each person finishes their meal, they cast off their mortal coil.

LeFranc was inspired to write *The Big Meal* after reading *The Long Christmas Dinner.*

Wilder writes in the notes to *The Long Christmas Dinner*, "Ninety years are traversed in this play which represents in accelerated motion ninety Christmas dinners in the Bayard hold. . . . Throughout the play the characters continue eating invisible food with invisible knives and forks. . . . There is no curtain."

Wilder found a way to both collapse and extend time, to locate the present moment onstage up against cosmic or mythic time. One can't really talk about Wilder without talking about time—the backdrop of Big Time up against the small moments of daily time. Roderick says, in *The Long Christmas Dinner*, "I'm going somewhere where time passes, my God!" His desire for time to pass is ironic—we are watching time move at hyperspeed.

I cannot remember when I first read *The Long Christmas Dinner.* I recently found a well-worn copy of the play in my office, the 1963 edition; my mother's maiden name, Kathleen A. Kehoe, was scrawled in script on the title page. Wilder believed in plays as literature, plays as books. Perhaps because Wilder was a consummate, incredibly successful novelist as well, the Book itself was very important to him. How lucky we are that he tacked between genres, sailing between them, gifting one genre with lessons from another.

Wilder said at one point that he was turning away from the novel and devoting himself entirely to plays because "drama is pure action without editorial comment and is closest to life since life itself is action without comment." Wilder no longer believed in the omniscient narrator, but he gave us unforgettable narrators onstage.

How do we stage the quiet, the interior, the invisible? Wilder showed us the way. When I was twenty, Paula Vogel told me to read the Belgian playwright Maurice Maeterlinck. I became obsessed with Maeterlinck and his descriptions of how to conjure the invisible onstage, which Wilder managed so uncannily. I was delighted to find, upon sleuthing with the help of Tappan Wilder, that Wilder also loved Maeterlinck, and even wrote a eulogy for him. This passage from the Belgian playwright's essay *The Tragical in Daily Life* could apply to most of Wilder's plays. Maeterlinck writes:

> It is almost only those words which at first appear unnecessary which give the work its value. It is in them that the soul may recognize itself.

I often tell my playwriting students to pay attention to dialogue that appears, in terms of plot, to be unnecessary—such seemingly unnecessary bits might be where the soul of the play resides. Maeterlinck lays out a dramaturgy that is based not on external conflict, but instead on revelations of the everyday spiritual life.

Wilder often makes fun of the demand for plot, both indirectly, in terms of what forms he chooses, and quite directly, referring to them as "these poor battered old plots . . ." (from *Such Things Only Happen in Books*). Like Wilder, Maurice Maeterlinck makes fun of conventional plots in drama that are romantic, swashbuckling, and violent, writing: "It is far away from bloodshed, battle-cry, and sword-thrust that the lives of most of us flow on; and men's tears are silent to-day, and invisible, and almost spiritual." Rereading Maeterlinck's passage about how to address the soul in the theater, I almost feel he could be writing about *Our Town*. Or *Pullman Car Hiawatha*, which is, in many ways, a rehearsal for *Our Town*. The Pullman train even passes through a field right next to Grover's Corners, in which there are "eight hundred twenty-one souls" (this Grover's Corners is in Ohio, not New Hampshire, where it will end up in *Our Town*). Everyone steeped in theater history knows Emily's goodbye speech, but they might not know Harriet's goodbye from the Pullman car:

> Good-bye, Philip. . . . Goodbye 1312 Ridgewood Avenue, Oaksbury, Illinois. I hope I remember all its steps and doors and wallpapers forever. Good-bye, Emerson Grammar School on the corner of Forbush Avenue and Wherry Street. Good-bye, Miss Walker and Miss Cramer who taught me English. . . . Good-bye, Papa and Mama. . . . Now I'm tired of saying good-bye.

This speech happens after Harriet has an argument with archangels; the angels silently intimate to Harriet that it's time to go.

Wilder wrote a little-known speech or essay called "The Barock; or, How to Recognize a Miracle in the Daily Life." Scholar Joseph Cermatori recently found it buried in Wilder's papers at the Beinecke Library—in the very same notebook in which Wilder wrote *Our Town*. Even the title—*a miracle in the daily life*—seems like a little nod to the Belgian playwright. In the essay, Wilder praises Baroque cosmology, which is less interested in representation, and more interested in the cosmic. He writes, "The Baroque is the art of seeing the Supernatural appearing continuously in the daily life."

And then Wilder asks a question that I found delightful, about the profusion of angels in Baroque art: "How do you paint an angel? Well, your ability to paint an angel *that is an angel* depends on the intensity with which you feel daily existence to be intermingled with the supernatural." *How do you paint an angel* indeed! How do you write the invisible? And how do you paint, or write, the afterlife? How can you *stage* memory?

In one great production of *Our Town* directed by David Cromer, the smell of bacon wafted into the theater when Emily visits her life again, and the whole audience, apparently, wept from the smell. The bacon trick reminds me of Maurice Maeterlinck's desire to make smell machines for the audience to appeal, on the most subtle level, to the sense most associated with memory. Wilder's plays do an end-run around the seen world, staging the invisible.

4.

Two people are sobbing behind me and clutching at each other, watching Noah Haidle's play *Birthday Candles* on Broadway. The play is the story of one woman's life told in ninety birthdays and many birthday cakes. The nod to *The Long Christmas Dinner* is clear in the particular choice of ninety years to be traversed onstage, and in the yearning to capture the existential universal. In an interview, Haidle says of Wilder and Beckett: "Their writing feels true in a way that other people's writing does not feel as true to me. . . . It's kind of like finding your family tree."

Again, the tree! I look at the little pinecone I took from Wilder's yard, which is now sitting on my desk.

Wilder writes in his preface to *Three Plays*, "The theatre has lagged behind the other arts in finding the 'new ways' to express how men and women think and feel in our time. I am not one of the new dramatists we are looking for. I wish I were. I hope I have played a part in preparing the way for them."

Of course, his humility is a bit silly; he was absolutely one of those new dramatists who changed everything. And yet, I appreciate his humility, especially compared with some other swaggering midcentury playwrights whose plays are often built on conflict. Wilder's plays are built on something else, something quieter—*if only we had paid more attention, if only we had been kinder*. . . . The emotion creeps up on the audience, unconscious, but then like a tidal wave, almost unbidden.

That Thornton Wilder always makes me cry—and not only his own work, but the work of my contemporaries whom he's *influenced*—isn't that extraordinary? And indeed, Wilder played a huge part in preparing the way for contemporary writers who look to his work for instructions on how to invent new forms, for tips on having access to an invisible world, on how to bend time, and on staging the interior. We look to Wilder for ways to distill, rather than to represent, life. His ability to toggle between emotion and abstraction, between the individual and the collective, gives his plays the feeling of being ancient and contemporary.

Wilder's plays give us the injunction to live more fully in the moment. They fairly leap off the page, telling us to wake up and live. Let's do just that.

Sarah Ruhl
Brooklyn, 2025

Our Town
A Play in Three Acts

To Alexander Woollcott
of Castleton Township, Rutland County, Vermont

The first performance of this play took place at the McCarter Theatre, Princeton, New Jersey, on January 22, 1938. The first New York performance was at Henry Miller's Theatre, February 4, 1938. It was produced and directed by Jed Harris. The technical director was Raymond Sovey; the costumes were designed by Madame Hélène Pons. The role of the Stage Manager was played by Frank Craven. The Gibbs family were played by Jay Fassett, Evelyn Varden, John Craven and Marilyn Erskine; the Webb family by Thomas Ross, Helen Carew, Martha Scott (as Emily) and Charles Wiley, Jr.; Mrs. Soames was played by Doro Merande; Simon Stimson by Philip Coolidge.

CHARACTERS (in the order of their appearance)

Stage Manager
Dr. Gibbs
Joe Crowell
Howie Newsome
Mrs. Gibbs
Mrs. Webb
George Gibbs
Rebecca Gibbs
Wally Webb
Emily Webb
Professor Willard
Mr. Webb
Woman in the Balcony
Man in the Auditorium
Lady in the Box
Simon Stimson
Mrs. Soames
Constable Warren
Si Crowell
Three Baseball Players
Sam Craig
Joe Stoddard

The entire play takes place in Grover's Corners, New Hampshire.

Act I

No curtain.

No scenery.

The audience, arriving, sees an empty stage in half-light.

Presently the STAGE MANAGER, *hat on and pipe in mouth, enters and begins placing a table and three chairs downstage left, and a table and three chairs downstage right.*

He also places a low bench at the corner of what will be the Webb house, left.

"Left" and "right" are from the point of view of the actor facing the audience. "Up" is toward the back wall.

As the house lights go down he has finished setting the stage and leaning against the right proscenium pillar watches the late arrivals in the audience.

When the auditorium is in complete darkness he speaks:

STAGE MANAGER:
This play is called "Our Town." It was written by Thornton Wilder; produced and directed by A. . . . (or: produced by A. . . . ; directed by B. . . .). In it you will see Miss C. . . . ; Miss D. . . . ; Miss E. . . . ; and Mr. F. . . . ; Mr. G. . . . ; Mr. H. . . . ; and many others. The name of the town is Grover's Corners, New Hampshire—just across the Massachusetts line: latitude 42 degrees 40 minutes; longitude 70 degrees 37 minutes. The First Act shows a day in our town. The day is May 7, 1901. The time is just before dawn.

A rooster crows.

The sky is beginning to show some streaks of light over in the East there, behind our mount'in.

The morning star always gets wonderful bright the minute before it has to go,—doesn't it?

He stares at it for a moment, then goes upstage.

Well, I'd better show you how our town lies. Up here—

That is: parallel with the back wall.

is Main Street. Way back there is the railway station; tracks go that way. Polish Town's across the tracks, and some Canuck families.

Toward the left.

Over there is the Congregational Church; across the street's the Presbyterian.

Methodist and Unitarian are over there.

Baptist is down in the holla' by the river.

Catholic Church is over beyond the tracks.

Here's the Town Hall and Post Office combined; jail's in the basement.

Bryan once made a speech from these very steps here.

Along here's a row of stores. Hitching posts and horse blocks in front of them. First automobile's going to come along in about five years—belonged to Banker Cartwright, our richest citizen . . . lives in the big white house up on the hill.

Here's the grocery store and here's Mr. Morgan's drugstore. Most everybody in town manages to look into those two stores once a day.

Public School's over yonder. High School's still farther over. Quarter of nine mornings, noontimes, and three o'clock afternoons, the hull town can hear the yelling and screaming from those schoolyards.

He approaches the table and chairs downstage right.

This is our doctor's house,—Doc Gibbs'. This is the back door.

Two arched trellises, covered with vines and flowers, are pushed out, one by each proscenium pillar.

There's some scenery for those who think they have to have scenery.

This is Mrs. Gibbs' garden. Corn . . . peas . . . beans . . . hollyhocks . . . heliotrope . . . and a lot of burdock.

Crosses the stage.

In those days our newspaper come out twice a week—the Grover's Corners *Sentinel*—and this is Editor Webb's house.

And this is Mrs. Webb's garden.

Just like Mrs. Gibbs', only it's got a lot of sunflowers, too.

He looks upward, center stage.

Right here . . .'s a big butternut tree.

He returns to his place by the right proscenium pillar and looks at the audience for a minute.

Nice town, y'know what I mean?

Nobody very remarkable ever come out of it, s'far as we know.

The earliest tombstones in the cemetery up there on the mountain say 1670–1680—they're Grovers and Cartwrights and Gibbses and Herseys—same names as are around here now.

Well, as I said: it's about dawn.

The only lights on in town are in a cottage over by the tracks where a Polish mother's just had twins. And in the Joe Crowell house, where Joe Junior's getting up so as to deliver the paper. And in the depot, where Shorty Hawkins is gettin' ready to flag the 5:45 for Boston.

A train whistle is heard. The STAGE MANAGER *takes out his watch and nods.*

Naturally, out in the country—all around—there've been lights on for some time, what with milkin's and so on. But town people sleep late.

So—another day's begun.

There's Doc Gibbs comin' down Main Street now, comin' back from that baby case. And here's his wife comin' downstairs to get breakfast.

MRS. GIBBS, *a plump, pleasant woman in the middle thirties, comes "downstairs" right. She pulls up an imaginary window shade in her kitchen and starts to make a fire in her stove.*

Doc Gibbs died in 1930. The new hospital's named after him.

Mrs. Gibbs died first—long time ago, in fact. She went out to visit her daughter, Rebecca, who married an insurance man in Canton, Ohio, and died there—pneumonia—but her body was brought back here. She's up in the cemetery there now—in with a whole mess of Gibbses and Herseys—she was Julia Hersey 'fore she married Doc Gibbs in the Congregational Church over there.

In our town we like to know the facts about everybody.

There's Mrs. Webb, coming downstairs to get her breakfast, too.

—That's Doc Gibbs. Got that call at half past one this morning.

And there comes Joe Crowell, Jr., delivering Mr. Webb's *Sentinel.*

DR. GIBBS *has been coming along Main Street from the left. At the point where he would turn to approach his house, he stops, sets down his—imaginary—black bag, takes off his hat, and rubs his face with fatigue, using an enormous handkerchief.*

MRS. WEBB, *a thin, serious, crisp woman, has entered her kitchen, left, tying on an apron. She goes through the motions of putting wood into a stove, lighting it, and preparing breakfast.*

Suddenly, JOE CROWELL, JR., *eleven, starts down Main Street from the right, hurling imaginary newspapers into doorways.*

JOE CROWELL, JR.:
Morning, Doc Gibbs.

DR. GIBBS:

Morning, Joe.

JOE CROWELL, JR.:

Somebody been sick, Doc?

DR. GIBBS:

No. Just some twins born over in Polish Town.

JOE CROWELL, JR.:

Do you want your paper now?

DR. GIBBS:

Yes, I'll take it.—Anything serious goin' on in the world since Wednesday?

JOE CROWELL, JR.:

Yessir. My schoolteacher, Miss Foster, 's getting married to a fella over in Concord.

DR. GIBBS:

I declare.—How do you boys feel about that?

JOE CROWELL, JR.:

Well, of course, it's none of my business—but I think if a person starts out to be a teacher, she ought to stay one.

DR. GIBBS:

How's your knee, Joe?

JOE CROWELL, JR.:

Fine, Doc, I never think about it at all. Only like you said, it always tells me when it's going to rain.

DR. GIBBS:
What's it telling you today? Goin' to rain?

JOE CROWELL, JR.:
No, sir.

DR. GIBBS:
Sure?

JOE CROWELL, JR.:
Yessir.

DR. GIBBS:
Knee ever make a mistake?

JOE CROWELL, JR.:
No, sir.

JOE *goes off.* DR. GIBBS *stands reading his paper.*

STAGE MANAGER:
Want to tell you something about that boy Joe Crowell there. Joe was awful bright—graduated from high school here, head of his class. So he got a scholarship to Massachusetts Tech. Graduated head of his class there, too. It was all wrote up in the Boston paper at the time. Goin' to be a great engineer, Joe was. But the war broke out and he died in France.—All that education for nothing.

HOWIE NEWSOME:
Off left.
Giddap, Bessie! What's the matter with you today?

STAGE MANAGER:
Here comes Howie Newsome, deliverin' the milk.

HOWIE NEWSOME, *about thirty, in overalls, comes along Main Street from the left, walking beside an invisible horse and wagon and carrying an imaginary rack with milk bottles. The sound of clinking milk bottles is heard. He leaves some bottles at Mrs. Webb's trellis, then, crossing the stage to Mrs. Gibbs', he stops center to talk to Dr. Gibbs.*

HOWIE NEWSOME:
Morning, Doc.

DR. GIBBS:
Morning, Howie.

HOWIE NEWSOME:
Somebody sick?

DR. GIBBS:
Pair of twins over to Mrs. Goruslawski's.

HOWIE NEWSOME:
Twins, eh? This town's gettin' bigger every year.

DR. GIBBS:
Goin' to rain, Howie?

HOWIE NEWSOME:
No, no. Fine day—that'll burn through. Come on, Bessie.

DR. GIBBS:
Hello Bessie.

He strokes the horse, which has remained up center.

How old is she, Howie?

HOWIE NEWSOME:

Going on seventeen. Bessie's all mixed up about the route ever since the Lockharts stopped takin' their quart of milk every day. She wants to leave 'em a quart just the same—keeps scolding me the hull trip.

He reaches Mrs. Gibbs' back door. She is waiting for him.

MRS. GIBBS:

Good morning, Howie.

HOWIE NEWSOME:

Morning, Mrs. Gibbs. Doc's just comin' down the street.

MRS. GIBBS:

Is he? Seems like you're late today.

HOWIE NEWSOME:

Yes. Somep'n went wrong with the separator. Don't know what 'twas.

He passes Dr. Gibbs up center.

Doc!

DR. GIBBS:

Howie!

MRS. GIBBS:

Calling upstairs.

Children! Children! Time to get up.

HOWIE NEWSOME:

Come on, Bessie!

He goes off right.

MRS. GIBBS:

George! Rebecca!

DR. GIBBS *arrives at his back door and passes through the trellis into his house.*

MRS. GIBBS:

Everything all right, Frank?

DR. GIBBS:

Yes. I declare—easy as kittens.

MRS. GIBBS:

Bacon'll be ready in a minute. Set down and drink your coffee. You can catch a couple hours' sleep this morning, can't you?

DR. GIBBS:

Hm! . . . Mrs. Wentworth's coming at eleven. Guess I know what it's about, too. Her stummick ain't what it ought to be.

MRS. GIBBS:

All told, you won't get more'n three hours' sleep. Frank Gibbs, I don't know what's goin' to become of you. I do wish I could get you to go away someplace and take a rest. I think it would do you good.

MRS. WEBB:

Emileeee! Time to get up! Wally! Seven o'clock!

MRS. GIBBS:

I declare, you got to speak to George. Seems like something's come over him lately. He's no help to me at all. I can't even get him to cut me some wood.

DR. GIBBS:

Washing and drying his hands at the sink. MRS. GIBBS *is busy at the stove.*

Is he sassy to you?

MRS. GIBBS:

No. He just whines! All he thinks about is that baseball—George! Rebecca! You'll be late for school.

DR. GIBBS:

M-m-m . . .

MRS. GIBBS:

George!

DR. GIBBS:

George, look sharp!

GEORGE'S VOICE:

Yes, Pa!

DR. GIBBS:

As he goes off the stage.

Don't you hear your mother calling you? I guess I'll go upstairs and get forty winks.

MRS. WEBB:
Walleee! Emileee! You'll be late for school! Walleee! You wash yourself good or I'll come up and do it myself.

REBECCA GIBBS' VOICE:
Ma! What dress shall I wear?

MRS. GIBBS:
Don't make a noise. Your father's been out all night and needs his sleep. I washed and ironed the blue gingham for you special.

REBECCA:
Ma, I hate that dress.

MRS. GIBBS:
Oh, hush-up-with-you.

REBECCA:
Every day I go to school dressed like a sick turkey.

MRS. GIBBS:
Now, Rebecca, you always look *very* nice.

REBECCA:
Mama, George's throwing soap at me.

MRS. GIBBS:
I'll come and slap the both of you,—that's what I'll do.

A factory whistle sounds.

The CHILDREN *dash in and take their places at the tables. Right,* GEORGE, *about sixteen, and* REBECCA, *eleven. Left,* EMILY *and* WALLY, *same ages. They carry strapped schoolbooks.*

STAGE MANAGER:
We've got a factory in our town too—hear it? Makes blankets. Cartwrights own it and it brung 'em a fortune.

MRS. WEBB:
Children! Now I won't have it. Breakfast is just as good as any other meal and I won't have you gobbling like wolves. It'll stunt your growth,—that's a fact. Put away your book, Wally.

WALLY:
Aw, Ma! By ten o'clock I got to know all about Canada.

MRS. WEBB:
You know the rule's well as I do—no books at table. As for me, I'd rather have my children healthy than bright.

EMILY:
I'm both, Mama: you know I am. I'm the brightest girl in school for my age. I have a wonderful memory.

MRS. WEBB:
Eat your breakfast.

WALLY:
I'm bright, too, when I'm looking at my stamp collection.

MRS. GIBBS:
I'll speak to your father about it when he's rested. Seems to me twenty-five cents a week's enough for a boy your age. I declare I don't know how you spend it all.

GEORGE:
Aw, Ma,—I gotta lotta things to buy.

MRS. GIBBS:
Strawberry phosphates—that's what you spend it on.

GEORGE:
I don't see how Rebecca comes to have so much money. She has more'n a dollar.

REBECCA:
Spoon in mouth, dreamily.
I've been saving it up gradual.

MRS. GIBBS:
Well, dear, I think it's a good thing to spend some every now and then.

REBECCA:
Mama, do you know what I love most in the world—do you?—Money.

MRS. GIBBS:
Eat your breakfast.

THE CHILDREN:
Mama, there's first bell.—I gotta hurry.—I don't want any more.—I gotta hurry.

The CHILDREN *rise, seize their books and dash out through the trellises. They meet, down center, and chattering, walk to Main Street, then turn left.*

The STAGE MANAGER *goes off, unobtrusively, right.*

MRS. WEBB:

Walk fast, but you don't have to run. Wally, pull up your pants at the knee. Stand up straight, Emily.

MRS. GIBBS:

Tell Miss Foster I send her my best congratulations—can you remember that?

REBECCA:

Yes, Ma.

MRS. GIBBS:

You look real nice, Rebecca. Pick up your feet.

ALL:

Good-by.

MRS. GIBBS *fills her apron with food for the chickens and comes down to the footlights.*

MRS. GIBBS:

Here, chick, chick, chick.

No, go away, you. Go away.

Here, chick, chick, chick.

What's the matter with *you*? Fight, fight, fight,—that's all you do.

Hm . . . *you* don't belong to me. Where'd you come from?

She shakes her apron.

Oh, don't be so scared. Nobody's going to hurt you.

MRS. WEBB *is sitting on the bench by her trellis, stringing beans.*

Good morning, Myrtle. How's your cold?

MRS. WEBB:

Well, I still get that tickling feeling in my throat. I told Charles I didn't know as I'd go to choir practice tonight. Wouldn't be any use.

MRS. GIBBS:

Have you tried singing over your voice?

MRS. WEBB:

Yes, but somehow I can't do that and stay on the key. While I'm resting myself I thought I'd string some of these beans.

MRS. GIBBS:

Rolling up her sleeves as she crosses the stage for a chat.

Let me help you. Beans have been good this year.

MRS. WEBB:

I've decided to put up forty quarts if it kills me. The children say they hate 'em, but I notice they're able to get 'em down all winter.

Pause. Brief sound of chickens cackling.

MRS. GIBBS:

Now, Myrtle. I've got to tell you something, because if I don't tell somebody I'll burst.

MRS. WEBB:

Why, Julia Gibbs!

MRS. GIBBS:

Here, give me some more of those beans. Myrtle, did one of those secondhand-furniture men from Boston come to see you last Friday?

MRS. WEBB:

No-o.

MRS. GIBBS:

Well, he called on me. First I thought he was a patient wantin' to see Dr. Gibbs. 'N he wormed his way into my parlor, and, Myrtle Webb, he offered me three hundred and fifty dollars for Grandmother Wentworth's highboy, as I'm sitting here!

MRS. WEBB:

Why, Julia Gibbs!

MRS. GIBBS:

He did! That old thing! Why, it was so big I didn't know where to put it and I almost give it to Cousin Hester Wilcox.

MRS. WEBB:

Well, you're going to take it, aren't you?

MRS. GIBBS:

I don't know.

MRS. WEBB:

You don't know—three hundred and fifty dollars! What's come over you?

MRS. GIBBS:

Well, if I could get the Doctor to take the money and go away someplace on a real trip, I'd sell it like that.—Y'know, Myrtle, it's been the dream of my life to see Paris, France.—Oh, I don't know. It sounds crazy, I suppose, but for years I've been promising myself that if we ever had the chance—

MRS. WEBB:
How does the Doctor feel about it?

MRS. GIBBS:
Well, I did beat about the bush a little and said that if I got a legacy—that's the way I put it—I'd make him take me somewhere.

MRS. WEBB:
M-m-m . . . What did he say?

MRS. GIBBS:
You know how he is. I haven't heard a serious word out of him since I've known him. No, he said, it might make him discontented with Grover's Corners to go traipsin' about Europe; better let well enough alone, he says. Every two years he makes a trip to the battlefields of the Civil War and that's enough treat for anybody, he says.

MRS. WEBB:
Well, Mr. Webb just *admires* the way Dr. Gibbs knows everything about the Civil War. Mr. Webb's a good mind to give up Napoleon and move over to the Civil War, only Dr. Gibbs being one of the greatest experts in the country just makes him despair.

MRS. GIBBS:
It's a fact! Dr. Gibbs is never so happy as when he's at Antietam or Gettysburg. The times I've walked over those hills, Myrtle, stopping at every bush and pacing it all out, like we were going to buy it.

MRS. WEBB:

Well, if that secondhand man's really serious about buyin' it, Julia, you sell it. And then you'll get to see Paris, all right. Just keep droppin' hints from time to time—that's how I got to see the Atlantic Ocean, y'know.

MRS. GIBBS:

Oh, I'm sorry I mentioned it. Only it seems to me that once in your life before you die you ought to see a country where they don't talk in English and don't even want to.

The STAGE MANAGER *enters briskly from the right. He tips his hat to the ladies, who nod their heads.*

STAGE MANAGER:

Thank you, ladies. Thank you very much.

MRS. GIBBS *and* MRS. WEBB *gather up their things, return into their homes and disappear.*

Now we're going to skip a few hours.

But first we want a little more information about the town, kind of a scientific account, you might say.

So I've asked Professor Willard of our State University to sketch in a few details of our past history here.

Is Professor Willard here?

PROFESSOR WILLARD, *a rural savant, pince-nez on a wide satin ribbon, enters from the right with some notes in his hand.*

May I introduce Professor Willard of our State University.

A few brief notes, thank you, Professor,—unfortunately our time is limited.

PROFESSOR WILLARD:

Grover's Corners . . . let me see . . . Grover's Corners lies on the old Pleistocene granite of the Appalachian range. I may say it's some of the oldest land in the world. We're very proud of that. A shelf of Devonian basalt crosses it with vestiges of Mesozoic shale, and some sandstone outcroppings; but that's all more recent: two hundred, three hundred million years old.

Some highly interesting fossils have been found . . . I may say: unique fossils . . . two miles out of town, in Silas Peckham's cow pasture. They can be seen at the museum in our University at any time—that is, at any reasonable time. Shall I read some of Professor Gruber's notes on the meteorological situation—mean precipitation, et cetera?

STAGE MANAGER:

Afraid we won't have time for that, Professor. We might have a few words on the history of man here.

PROFESSOR WILLARD:

Yes . . . anthropological data: Early Amerindian stock. Cotahatchee tribes . . . no evidence before the tenth century of this era . . . hm . . . now entirely disappeared . . . possible traces in three families. Migration toward the end of the seventeenth century of English brachiocephalic blue-eyed stock . . . for the most part. Since then some Slav and Mediterranean—

STAGE MANAGER:

And the population, Professor Willard?

PROFESSOR WILLARD:

Within the town limits: 2,640.

STAGE MANAGER:

Just a moment, Professor.

He whispers into the professor's ear.

PROFESSOR WILLARD:

Oh, yes, indeed?—The population, *at the moment,* is 2,642. The Postal District brings in 507 more, making a total of 3,149.—Mortality and birth rates: constant.—By MacPherson's gauge: 6.032.

STAGE MANAGER:

Thank you very much, Professor. We're all very much obliged to you, I'm sure.

PROFESSOR WILLARD:

Not at all, sir; not at all.

STAGE MANAGER:

This way, Professor, and thank you again.

Exit PROFESSOR WILLARD.

Now the political and social report: Editor Webb.—Oh, Mr. Webb?

MRS. WEBB *appears at her back door.*

MRS. WEBB:

He'll be here in a minute. . . . He just cut his hand while he was eatin' an apple.

STAGE MANAGER:

Thank you, Mrs. Webb.

MRS. WEBB:
Charles! Everybody's waitin'.

Exit MRS. WEBB.

STAGE MANAGER:
Mr. Webb is Publisher and Editor of the Grover's Corners *Sentinel.* That's our local paper, y'know.

MR. WEBB *enters from his house, pulling on his coat. His finger is bound in a handkerchief.*

MR. WEBB:
Well . . . I don't have to tell you that we're run here by a Board of Selectmen.—All males vote at the age of twenty-one. Women vote indirect. We're lower middle class: sprinkling of professional men . . . ten per cent illiterate laborers. Politically, we're eighty-six per cent Republicans; six per cent Democrats; four per cent Socialists; rest, indifferent.

Religiously, we're eighty-five per cent Protestants; twelve per cent Catholics; rest, indifferent.

STAGE MANAGER:
Have you any comments, Mr. Webb?

MR. WEBB:
Very ordinary town, if you ask me. Little better behaved than most. Probably a lot duller.

But our young people here seem to like it well enough. Ninety per cent of 'em graduating from high school settle down right here to live—even when they've been away to college.

STAGE MANAGER:
Now, is there anyone in the audience who would like to ask Editor Webb anything about the town?

WOMAN IN THE BALCONY:
Is there much drinking in Grover's Corners?

MR. WEBB:
Well, ma'am, I wouldn't know what you'd call *much.* Satiddy nights the farmhands meet down in Ellery Greenough's stable and holler some. We've got one or two town drunks, but they're always having remorses every time an evangelist comes to town. No, ma'am, I'd say likker ain't a regular thing in the home here, except in the medicine chest. Right good for snake bite, y'know—always was.

BELLIGERENT MAN AT BACK OF AUDITORIUM:
Is there no one in town aware of—

STAGE MANAGER:
Come forward, will you, where we can all hear you—What were you saying?

BELLIGERENT MAN:
Is there no one in town aware of social injustice and industrial inequality?

MR. WEBB:
Oh, yes, everybody is—somethin' terrible. Seems like they spend most of their time talking about who's rich and who's poor.

BELLIGERENT MAN:
Then why don't they do something about it?

He withdraws without waiting for an answer.

MR. WEBB:

Well, I dunno. . . . I guess we're all hunting like everybody else for a way the diligent and sensible can rise to the top and the lazy and quarrelsome can sink to the bottom. But it ain't easy to find. Meanwhile, we do all we can to help those that can't help themselves and those that can we leave alone.—Are there any other questions?

LADY IN A BOX:

Oh, Mr. Webb? Mr. Webb, is there any culture or love of beauty in Grover's Corners?

MR. WEBB:

Well, ma'am, there ain't much—not in the sense you mean. Come to think of it, there's some girls that play the piano at High School Commencement; but they ain't happy about it. No, ma'am, there isn't much culture; but maybe this is the place to tell you that we've got a lot of pleasures of a kind here: we like the sun comin' up over the mountain in the morning, and we all notice a good deal about the birds. We pay a lot of attention to them. And we watch the change of the seasons; yes, everybody knows about them. But those other things—you're right, ma'am,—there ain't much.—*Robinson Crusoe* and the Bible; and Handel's "Largo," we all know that; and Whistler's "Mother"—those are just about as far as we go.

LADY IN A BOX:

So I thought. Thank you, Mr. Webb.

STAGE MANAGER:

Thank you, Mr. Webb.

MR. WEBB *retires.*

Now, we'll go back to the town. It's early afternoon. All 2,642 have had their dinners and all the dishes have been washed.

MR. WEBB, *having removed his coat, returns and starts pushing a lawn mower to and fro beside his house.*

There's an early-afternoon calm in our town: a buzzin' and a hummin' from the school buildings; only a few buggies on Main Street—the horses dozing at the hitching posts; you all remember what it's like. Doc Gibbs is in his office, tapping people and making them say "ah." Mr. Webb's cuttin' his lawn over there; one man in ten thinks it's a privilege to push his own lawn mower.

No, sir. It's later than I thought. There are the children coming home from school already.

Shrill girls' voices are heard, off left. EMILY *comes along Main Street, carrying some books. There are some signs that she is imagining herself to be a lady of startling elegance.*

EMILY:

I *can't*, Lois. I've got to go home and help my mother. I *promised.*

MR. WEBB:

Emily, walk simply. Who do you think you are today?

EMILY:

Papa, you're terrible. One minute you tell me to stand up straight and the next minute you call me names. I just don't listen to you.

She gives him an abrupt kiss.

MR. WEBB:

Golly, I never got a kiss from such a great lady before.

He goes out of sight. EMILY *leans over and picks some flowers by the gate of her house.*

GEORGE GIBBS *comes careening down Main Street. He is throwing a ball up to dizzying heights, and waiting to catch it again. This sometimes requires his taking six steps backward. He bumps into an* OLD LADY *invisible to us.*

GEORGE:
Excuse me, Mrs. Forrest.

STAGE MANAGER:
As Mrs. Forrest.

Go out and play in the fields, young man. You got no business playing baseball on Main Street.

GEORGE:
Awfully sorry, Mrs. Forrest.—Hello, Emily.

EMILY:
H'lo.

GEORGE:
You made a fine speech in class.

EMILY:
Well . . . I was really ready to make a speech about the Monroe Doctrine, but at the last minute Miss Corcoran made me talk about the Louisiana Purchase instead. I worked an awful long time on both of them.

GEORGE:
Gee, it's funny, Emily. From my window up there I can just see your head nights when you're doing your homework over in your room.

EMILY:
Why, can you?

GEORGE:
You certainly do stick to it, Emily. I don't see how you can sit still that long. I guess you like school.

EMILY:
Well, I always feel it's something you have to go through.

GEORGE:
Yeah.

EMILY:
I don't mind it really. It passes the time.

GEORGE:
Yeah.—Emily, what do you think? We might work out a kinda telegraph from your window to mine; and once in a while you could give me a kinda hint or two about one of those algebra problems. I don't mean the answers, Emily, of course not . . . just some little hint . . .

EMILY:
Oh, I think *hints* are allowed.—So—ah—if you get stuck, George, you whistle to me; and I'll give you some hints.

GEORGE:
Emily, you're just naturally bright, I guess.

EMILY:
I figure that it's just the way a person's born.

GEORGE:
Yeah. But, you see, I want to be a farmer, and my Uncle Luke says

whenever I'm ready I can come over and work on his farm and if I'm any good I can just gradually have it.

EMILY:
You mean the house and everything?

Enter MRS. WEBB *with a large bowl and sits on the bench by her trellis.*

GEORGE:
Yeah. Well, thanks . . . I better be getting out to the baseball field. Thanks for the talk, Emily.—Good afternoon, Mrs. Webb.

MRS. WEBB:
Good afternoon, George.

GEORGE:
So long, Emily.

EMILY:
So long, George.

MRS. WEBB:
Emily, come and help me string these beans for the winter. George Gibbs let himself have a real conversation, didn't he? Why, he's growing up. How old would George be?

EMILY:
I don't know.

MRS. WEBB:
Let's see. He must be almost sixteen.

EMILY:
Mama, I made a speech in class today and I was very good.

MRS. WEBB:

You must recite it to your father at supper. What was it about?

EMILY:

The Louisiana Purchase. It was like silk off a spool. I'm going to make speeches all my life.—Mama, are these big enough?

MRS. WEBB:

Try and get them a little bigger if you can.

EMILY:

Mama, will you answer me a question, serious?

MRS. WEBB:

Seriously, dear—not serious.

EMILY:

Seriously,—will you?

MRS. WEBB:

Of course, I will.

EMILY:

Mama, am I good looking?

MRS. WEBB:

Yes, of course you are. All my children have got good features; I'd be ashamed if they hadn't.

EMILY:

Oh, Mama, that's not what I mean. What I mean is: am I *pretty*?

MRS. WEBB:

I've already told you, yes. Now that's enough of that. You have a nice young pretty face. I never heard of such foolishness.

EMILY:
Oh, Mama, you never tell us the truth about anything.

MRS. WEBB:
I *am* telling you the truth.

EMILY:
Mama, were *you* pretty?

MRS. WEBB:
Yes, I was, if I do say it. I was the prettiest girl in town next to Mamie Cartwright.

EMILY:
But, Mama, you've got to say *something* about me. Am I pretty enough . . . to get anybody . . . to get people interested in me?

MRS. WEBB:
Emily, you make me tired. Now stop it. You're pretty enough for all normal purposes.—Come along now and bring that bowl with you.

EMILY:
Oh, Mama, you're no help at all.

STAGE MANAGER:
Thank you. Thank you! That'll do. We'll have to interrupt again here. Thank you, Mrs. Webb; thank you, Emily.

MRS. WEBB *and* EMILY *withdraw.*

There are some more things we want to explore about this town.

He comes to the center of the stage. During the following speech the lights gradually dim to darkness, leaving only a spot on him.

I think this is a good time to tell you that the Cartwright interests have just begun building a new bank in Grover's Corners—had to go to Vermont for the marble, sorry to say. And they've asked a friend of mine what they should put in the cornerstone for people to dig up . . . a thousand years from now. . . . Of course, they've put in a copy of the *New York Times* and a copy of Mr. Webb's *Sentinel*. . . . We're kind of interested in this because some scientific fellas have found a way of painting all that reading matter with a glue—a silicate glue—that'll make it keep a thousand—two thousand years.

We're putting in a Bible . . . and the Constitution of the United States—and a copy of William Shakespeare's plays. What do you say, folks? What do you think?

Y'know—Babylon once had two million people in it, and all we know about 'em is the names of the kings and some copies of wheat contracts . . . and contracts for the sale of slaves. Yet every night all those families sat down to supper, and the father came home from his work, and the smoke went up the chimney,—same as here. And even in Greece and Rome, all we know about the *real* life of the people is what we can piece together out of the joking poems and the comedies they wrote for the theatre back then.

So I'm going to have a copy of this play put in the cornerstone and the people a thousand years from now'll know a few simple facts about us—more than the Treaty of Versailles and the Lindbergh flight.

See what I mean?

So—people a thousand years from now—this is the way we were in the provinces north of New York at the beginning of the twentieth century.—This is the way we were: in our growing up and in our marrying and in our living and in our dying.

A choir partially concealed in the orchestra pit has begun singing "Blessed Be the Tie That Binds."

SIMON STIMSON *stands directing them.*

Two ladders have been pushed onto the stage; they serve as indication of the second story in the Gibbs and Webb houses. GEORGE *and* EMILY *mount them, and apply themselves to their schoolwork.*

DR. GIBBS *has entered and is seated in his kitchen reading.*

Well!—good deal of time's gone by. It's evening.

You can hear choir practice going on in the Congregational Church.

The children are at home doing their schoolwork.

The day's running down like a tired clock.

SIMON STIMSON:
Now look here, everybody. Music come into the world to give pleasure.—Softer! Softer! Get it out of your heads that music's only good when it's loud. You leave loudness to the Methodists. You couldn't beat 'em, even if you wanted to. Now again. Tenors!

GEORGE:
Hssst! Emily!

EMILY:
Hello.

GEORGE:
Hello!

EMILY:

I can't work at all. The moonlight's so *terrible.*

GEORGE:

Emily, did you get the third problem?

EMILY:

Which?

GEORGE:

The *third?*

EMILY:

Why, yes, George—that's the easiest of them all.

GEORGE:

I don't see it. Emily, can you give me a hint?

EMILY:

I'll tell you one thing: the answer's in yards.

GEORGE:

!!! In yards? How do you mean?

EMILY:

In *square* yards.

GEORGE:

Oh . . . in square yards.

EMILY:

Yes, George, don't you see?

GEORGE:

Yeah.

EMILY:

In square yards of *wallpaper*.

GEORGE:

Wallpaper,—oh, I see. Thanks a lot, Emily.

EMILY:

You're welcome. My, isn't the moonlight *terrible*? And choir practice going on.—I think if you hold your breath you can hear the train all the way to Contoocook. Hear it?

GEORGE:

M-m-m—What do you know!

EMILY:

Well, I guess I better go back and try to work.

GEORGE:

Good night, Emily. And thanks.

EMILY:

Good night, George.

SIMON STIMSON:

Before I forget it: how many of you will be able to come in Tuesday afternoon and sing at Fred Hersey's wedding?—show your hands. That'll be fine; that'll be right nice. We'll do the same music we did for Jane Trowbridge's last month.

—Now we'll do: "Art Thou Weary; Art Thou Languid?" It's a question, ladies and gentlemen, make it talk. Ready.

DR. GIBBS:

Oh, George, can you come down a minute?

GEORGE:

Yes, Pa.

He descends the ladder.

DR. GIBBS:

Make yourself comfortable, George; I'll only keep you a minute. George, how old are you?

GEORGE:

I? I'm sixteen, almost seventeen.

DR. GIBBS:

What do you want to do after school's over?

GEORGE:

Why, you know, Pa. I want to be a farmer on Uncle Luke's farm.

DR. GIBBS:

You'll be willing, will you, to get up early and milk and feed the stock . . . and you'll be able to hoe and hay all day?

GEORGE:

Sure, I will. What are you . . . what do you mean, Pa?

DR. GIBBS:

Well, George, while I was in my office today I heard a funny sound . . . and what do you think it was? It was your mother chopping wood. There you see your mother—getting up early; cooking meals all day long; washing and ironing;—and still she has to go out in the back yard and chop wood. I suppose she just got tired of asking you. She just gave up and decided it was easier to do it herself. And you eat her meals, and put on the clothes she keeps nice for you, and you run off and play baseball,—like she's some hired girl we keep around the house but that we don't like very much. Well, I knew all I had to do was call your attention to it. Here's a handkerchief, son. George, I've decided to raise your spending money twenty-five cents a week. Not, of course, for chopping wood for your mother, because that's a present you give her, but because you're getting older—and I imagine there are lots of things you must find to do with it.

GEORGE:
Thanks, Pa.

DR. GIBBS:
Let's see—tomorrow's your payday. You can count on it—Hmm. Probably Rebecca'll feel she ought to have some more too. Wonder what could have happened to your mother. Choir practice never was as late as this before.

GEORGE:
It's only half past eight, Pa.

DR. GIBBS:
I don't know why she's in that old choir. She hasn't any more voice than an old crow. . . . Traipsin' around the streets at this hour of the night . . . Just about time you retired, don't you think?

GEORGE:
Yes, Pa.

GEORGE *mounts to his place on the ladder.*

Laughter and good nights can be heard on stage left and presently MRS. GIBBS, MRS. SOAMES *and* MRS. WEBB *come down Main Street. When they arrive at the corner of the stage they stop.*

MRS. SOAMES:
Good night, Martha. Good night, Mr. Foster.

MRS. WEBB:
I'll tell Mr. Webb; I *know* he'll want to put it in the paper.

MRS. GIBBS:
My, it's late!

MRS. SOAMES:
Good night, Irma.

MRS. GIBBS:
Real nice choir practice, wa'n't it? Myrtle Webb! Look at that moon, will you! Tsk-tsk-tsk. Potato weather, for sure.

They are silent a moment, gazing up at the moon.

MRS. SOAMES:
Naturally I didn't want to say a word about it in front of those others, but now we're alone—really, it's the worst scandal that ever was in this town!

MRS. GIBBS:
What?

MRS. SOAMES:
Simon Stimson!

MRS. GIBBS:
Now, Louella!

MRS. SOAMES:
But, Julia! To have the organist of a church *drink* and *drunk* year after year. You know he was drunk tonight.

MRS. GIBBS:
Now, Louella! We all know about Mr. Stimson, and we all know about the troubles he's been through, and Dr. Ferguson knows too, and if Dr. Ferguson keeps him on there in his job the only thing the rest of us can do is just not to notice it.

MRS. SOAMES:
Not to notice it! But it's getting worse.

MRS. WEBB:
No, it isn't, Louella. It's getting better. I've been in that choir twice as long as you have. It doesn't happen anywhere near so often. . . . My, I hate to go to bed on a night like this.—I better hurry. Those children'll be sitting up till all hours. Good night, Louella.

They all exchange good nights. She hurries downstage, enters her house and disappears.

MRS. GIBBS:
Can you get home safe, Louella?

MRS. SOAMES:
It's as bright as day. I can see Mr. Soames scowling at the window now. You'd think we'd been to a dance the way the menfolk carry on.

More good nights. MRS. GIBBS *arrives at her home and passes through the trellis into the kitchen.*

MRS. GIBBS:
Well, we had a real good time.

DR. GIBBS:
You're late enough.

MRS. GIBBS:
Why, Frank, it ain't any later 'n usual.

DR. GIBBS:
And you stopping at the corner to gossip with a lot of hens.

MRS. GIBBS:
Now, Frank, don't be grouchy. Come out and smell the heliotrope in the moonlight.

They stroll out arm in arm along the footlights.

Isn't that wonderful? What did you do all the time I was away?

DR. GIBBS:
Oh, I read—as usual. What were the girls gossiping about tonight?

MRS. GIBBS:
Well, believe me, Frank—there is something to gossip about.

DR. GIBBS:
Hmm! Simon Stimson far gone, was he?

MRS. GIBBS:
Worst I've ever seen him. How'll that end, Frank? Dr. Ferguson can't forgive him forever.

DR. GIBBS:
I guess I know more about Simon Stimson's affairs than anybody in this town. Some people ain't made for small-town life. I don't know how that'll end; but there's nothing we can do but just leave it alone. Come, get in.

MRS. GIBBS:

No, not yet . . . Frank, I'm worried about you.

DR. GIBBS:

What are you worried about?

MRS. GIBBS:

I think it's my duty to make plans for you to get a real rest and change. And if I get that legacy, well, I'm going to insist on it.

DR. GIBBS:

Now, Julia, there's no sense in going over that again.

MRS. GIBBS:

Frank, you're just *unreasonable!*

DR. GIBBS:

Starting into the house.

Come on, Julia, it's getting late. First thing you know you'll catch cold. I gave George a piece of my mind tonight. I reckon you'll have your wood chopped for a while anyway. No, no, start getting upstairs.

MRS. GIBBS:

Oh, dear. There's always so many things to pick up, seems like. You know, Frank, Mrs. Fairchild always locks her front door every night. All those people up that part of town do.

DR. GIBBS:

Blowing out the lamp.

They're all getting citified, that's the trouble with them. They haven't got nothing fit to burgle and everybody knows it.

They disappear.

REBECCA *climbs up the ladder beside* GEORGE.

GEORGE:

Get out, Rebecca. There's only room for one at this window. You're always spoiling everything.

REBECCA:

Well, let me look just a minute.

GEORGE:

Use your own window.

REBECCA:

I did, but there's no moon there. . . . George, do you know what I think, do you? I think maybe the moon's getting nearer and nearer and there'll be a big 'splosion.

GEORGE:

Rebecca, you don't know anything. If the moon were getting nearer, the guys that sit up all night with telescopes would see it first and they'd tell about it, and it'd be in all the newspapers.

REBECCA:

George, is the moon shining on South America, Canada and half the whole world?

GEORGE:

Well—prob'ly is.

The STAGE MANAGER *strolls on.*

Pause. The sound of crickets is heard.

STAGE MANAGER:

Nine thirty. Most of the lights are out. No, there's Constable Warren trying a few doors on Main Street. And here comes Editor Webb, after putting his newspaper to bed.

MR. WARREN, *an elderly policeman, comes along Main Street from the right*, MR. WEBB *from the left.*

MR. WEBB:

Good evening, Bill.

CONSTABLE WARREN:

Evenin', Mr. Webb.

MR. WEBB:

Quite a moon!

CONSTABLE WARREN:

Yepp.

MR. WEBB:

All quiet tonight?

CONSTABLE WARREN:

Simon Stimson is rollin' around a little. Just saw his wife movin' out to hunt for him so I looked the other way—there he is now.

SIMON STIMSON *comes down Main Street from the left, only a trace of unsteadiness in his walk.*

MR. WEBB:

Good evening, Simon . . . Town seems to have settled down for the night pretty well. . . .

SIMON STIMSON *comes up to him and pauses a moment and stares at him, swaying slightly.*

Good evening . . . Yes, most of the town's settled down for the night, Simon. . . . I guess we better do the same. Can I walk along a ways with you?

SIMON STIMSON *continues on his way without a word and disappears at the right.*

Good night.

CONSTABLE WARREN:
I don't know how that's goin' to end, Mr. Webb.

MR. WEBB:
Well, he's seen a peck of trouble, one thing after another. . . . Oh, Bill . . . if you see my boy smoking cigarettes, just give him a word, will you? He thinks a lot of you, Bill.

CONSTABLE WARREN:
I don't think he smokes no cigarettes, Mr. Webb. Leastways, not more'n two or three a year.

MR. WEBB:
Hm . . . I hope not.—Well, good night, Bill.

CONSTABLE WARREN:
Good night, Mr. Webb.

Exit.

MR. WEBB:
Who's that up there? Is that you, Myrtle?

EMILY:
No, it's me, Papa.

MR. WEBB:
Why aren't you in bed?

EMILY:
I don't know. I just can't sleep yet, Papa. The moonlight's so *won*-derful. And the smell of Mrs. Gibbs' heliotrope. Can you smell it?

MR. WEBB:
Hm . . . Yes. Haven't any troubles on your mind, have you, Emily?

EMILY:
Troubles, Papa? *No.*

MR. WEBB:
Well, enjoy yourself, but don't let your mother catch you. Good night, Emily.

EMILY:
Good night, Papa.

MR. WEBB *crosses into the house, whistling "Blessed Be the Tie That Binds" and disappears.*

REBECCA:
I never told you about that letter Jane Crofut got from her minister when she was sick. He wrote Jane a letter and on the envelope the address was like this: It said: Jane Crofut; The Crofut Farm; Grover's Corners; Sutton County; New Hampshire; United States of America.

GEORGE:

What's funny about that?

REBECCA:

But listen, it's not finished: the United States of America; Continent of North America; Western Hemisphere; the Earth; the Solar System; the Universe; the Mind of God—that's what it said on the envelope.

GEORGE:

What do you know!

REBECCA:

And the postman brought it just the same.

GEORGE:

What do you know!

STAGE MANAGER:

That's the end of the First Act, friends. You can go and smoke now, those that smoke.

Act II

The tables and chairs of the two kitchens are still on the stage.

The ladders and the small bench have been withdrawn.

The STAGE MANAGER *has been at his accustomed place watching the audience return to its seats.*

STAGE MANAGER:

Three years have gone by.

Yes, the sun's come up over a thousand times.

Summers and winters have cracked the mountains a little bit more and the rains have brought down some of the dirt.

Some babies that weren't even born before have begun talking regular sentences already; and a number of people who thought they were right young and spry have noticed that they can't bound up a flight of stairs like they used to, without their heart fluttering a little.

All that can happen in a thousand days.

Nature's been pushing and contriving in other ways, too: a number of young people fell in love and got married.

Yes, the mountain got bit away a few fractions of an inch; millions of gallons of water went by the mill; and here and there a new home was set up under a roof.

Almost everybody in the world gets married,—you know what I mean? In our town there aren't hardly any exceptions. Most everybody in the world climbs into their graves married.

The First Act was called the Daily Life. This act is called Love and Marriage. There's another act coming after this: I reckon you can guess what that's about.

So:

It's three years later. It's 1904.

It's July 7th, just after High School Commencement.

That's the time most of our young people jump up and get married.

Soon as they've passed their last examinations in solid geometry and Cicero's Orations, looks like they suddenly feel themselves fit to be married.

It's early morning. Only this time it's been raining. It's been pouring and thundering.

Mrs. Gibbs' garden, and Mrs. Webb's here: drenched.

All those bean poles and pea vines: drenched.

All yesterday over there on Main Street, the rain looked like curtains being blown along.

Hm . . . it may begin again any minute.

There! You can hear the 5:45 for Boston.

MRS. GIBBS *and* MRS. WEBB *enter their kitchens and start the day as in the First Act.*

And there's Mrs. Gibbs and Mrs. Webb come down to make breakfast, just as though it were an ordinary day. I don't have to point out to the women in my audience that those ladies they see before them, both of those ladies cooked three meals a day—one of 'em for twenty years, the other for forty—and no summer vacation. They brought up two children apiece, washed, cleaned the house,—and *never a nervous breakdown.*

It's like what one of those Middle West poets said: You've got to love life to have life, and you've got to have life to love life. . . . It's what they call a vicious circle.

HOWIE NEWSOME:
Off stage left.

Giddap, Bessie!

STAGE MANAGER:
Here comes Howie Newsome delivering the milk. And there's Si Crowell delivering the papers like his brother before him.

SI CROWELL *has entered hurling imaginary newspapers into doorways;* HOWIE NEWSOME *has come along Main Street with Bessie.*

SI CROWELL:
Morning, Howie.

HOWIE NEWSOME:
Morning, Si.—Anything in the papers I ought to know?

SI CROWELL:
Nothing much, except we're losing about the best baseball pitcher Grover's Corners ever had—George Gibbs.

HOWIE NEWSOME:
Reckon he is.

SI CROWELL:
He could hit and run bases, too.

HOWIE NEWSOME:
Yep. Mighty fine ball player.—Whoa! Bessie! I guess I can stop and talk if I've a mind to!

SI CROWELL:
I don't see how he could give up a thing like that just to get married. Would you, Howie?

HOWIE NEWSOME:
Can't tell, Si. Never had no talent that way.

CONSTABLE WARREN *enters. They exchange good mornings.*

You're up early, Bill.

CONSTABLE WARREN:
Seein' if there's anything I can do to prevent a flood. River's been risin' all night.

HOWIE NEWSOME:
Si Crowell's all worked up here about George Gibbs' retiring from baseball.

CONSTABLE WARREN:

Yes, sir; that's the way it goes. Back in '84 we had a player, Si—even George Gibbs couldn't touch him. Name of Hank Todd. Went down to Maine and become a parson. Wonderful ball player.—Howie, how does the weather look to you?

HOWIE NEWSOME:

Oh, 'tain't bad. Think maybe it'll clear up for good.

CONSTABLE WARREN *and* SI CROWELL *continue on their way.*

HOWIE NEWSOME *brings the milk first to Mrs. Gibbs' house. She meets him by the trellis.*

MRS. GIBBS:

Good morning, Howie. Do you think it's going to rain again?

HOWIE NEWSOME:

Morning, Mrs. Gibbs. It rained so heavy, I think maybe it'll clear up.

MRS. GIBBS:

Certainly hope it will.

HOWIE NEWSOME:

How much did you want today?

MRS. GIBBS:

I'm going to have a houseful of relations, Howie. Looks to me like I'll need three-a-milk and two-a-cream.

HOWIE NEWSOME:

My wife says to tell you we both hope they'll be very happy, Mrs. Gibbs. Know they *will.*

MRS. GIBBS:

Thanks a lot, Howie. Tell your wife I hope she gits there to the wedding.

HOWIE NEWSOME:

Yes, she'll be there; she'll be there if she kin.

HOWIE NEWSOME *crosses to Mrs. Webb's house.*

Morning, Mrs. Webb.

MRS. WEBB:

Oh, good morning, Mr. Newsome. I told you four quarts of milk, but I hope you can spare me another.

HOWIE NEWSOME:

Yes'm . . . and the two of cream.

MRS. WEBB:

Will it start raining again, Mr. Newsome?

HOWIE NEWSOME:

Well. Just sayin' to Mrs. Gibbs as how it may lighten up. Mrs. Newsome told me to tell you as how we hope they'll both be very happy, Mrs. Webb. Know they *will.*

MRS. WEBB:

Thank you, and thank Mrs. Newsome and we're counting on seeing you at the wedding.

HOWIE NEWSOME:

Yes, Mrs. Webb. We hope to git there. Couldn't miss that. Come on, Bessie.

Exit HOWIE NEWSOME.

DR. GIBBS *descends in shirt sleeves, and sits down at his breakfast table.*

DR. GIBBS:

Well, Ma, the day has come. You're losin' one of your chicks.

MRS. GIBBS:

Frank Gibbs, don't you say another word. I feel like crying every minute. Sit down and drink your coffee.

DR. GIBBS:

The groom's up shaving himself—only there ain't an awful lot to shave. Whistling and singing, like he's glad to leave us.—Every now and then he says "I do" to the mirror, but it don't sound convincing to me.

MRS. GIBBS:

I declare, Frank, I don't know how he'll get along. I've arranged his clothes and seen to it he's put warm things on,—Frank! they're too *young*. Emily won't think of such things. He'll catch his death of cold within a week.

DR. GIBBS:

I was remembering my wedding morning, Julia.

MRS. GIBBS:

Now don't start that, Frank Gibbs.

DR. GIBBS:

I was the scaredest young fella in the State of New Hampshire. I thought I'd make a mistake for sure. And when I saw you comin' down that aisle I thought you were the prettiest girl

I'd ever seen, but the only trouble was that I'd never seen you before. There I was in the Congregational Church marryin' a total stranger.

MRS. GIBBS:
And how do you think I felt!—Frank, weddings are perfectly awful things. Farces,—that's what they are!

She puts a plate before him.

Here, I've made something for you.

DR. GIBBS:
Why, Julia Hersey—French toast!

MRS. GIBBS:
'Tain't hard to make and I had to do *some*thing.

Pause. DR. GIBBS *pours on the syrup.*

DR. GIBBS:
How'd you sleep last night, Julia?

MRS. GIBBS:
Well, I heard a lot of the hours struck off.

DR. GIBBS:
Ye-e-s! I get a shock every time I think of George setting out to be a family man—that great gangling thing!—I tell you, Julia, there's nothing so terrifying in the world as a *son*. The relation of father and son is the darndest, awkwardest—

MRS. GIBBS:
Well, mother and daughter's no picnic, let me tell you.

DR. GIBBS:

They'll have a lot of troubles, I suppose, but that's none of our business. Everybody has a right to their own troubles.

MRS. GIBBS:

At the table, drinking her coffee, meditatively.

Yes . . . people are meant to go through life two by two. 'Tain't natural to be lonesome.

Pause. DR. GIBBS *starts laughing.*

DR. GIBBS:

Julia, do you know one of the things I was scared of when I married you?

MRS. GIBBS:

Oh, go along with you!

DR. GIBBS:

I was afraid we wouldn't have material for conversation more'n'd last us a few weeks.

Both laugh.

I was afraid we'd run out and eat our meals in silence, that's a fact.—Well, you and I been conversing for twenty years now without any noticeable barren spells.

MRS. GIBBS:

Well,—good weather, bad weather—'tain't very choice, but I always find something to say.

She goes to the foot of the stairs.

Did you hear Rebecca stirring around upstairs?

DR. GIBBS:

No. Only day of the year Rebecca hasn't been managing everybody's business up there. She's hiding in her room.—I got the impression she's crying.

MRS. GIBBS:

Lord's sakes!—This has got to stop.—Rebecca! Rebecca! Come and get your breakfast.

GEORGE *comes rattling down the stairs, very brisk.*

GEORGE:

Good morning, everybody. Only five more hours to live.

Makes the gesture of cutting his throat, and a loud "k-k-k," and starts through the trellis.

MRS. GIBBS:

George Gibbs, where are you going?

GEORGE:

Just stepping across the grass to see my girl.

MRS. GIBBS:

Now, George! You put on your overshoes. It's raining torrents. You don't go out of this house without you're prepared for it.

GEORGE:

Aw, Ma. It's just a *step!*

MRS. GIBBS:

George! You'll catch your death of cold and cough all through the service.

DR. GIBBS:

George, do as your mother tells you!

DR. GIBBS *goes upstairs.*

GEORGE *returns reluctantly to the kitchen and pantomimes putting on overshoes.*

MRS. GIBBS:

From tomorrow on you can kill yourself in all weathers, but while you're in my house you'll live wisely, thank you.—Maybe Mrs. Webb isn't used to callers at seven in the morning.—Here, take a cup of coffee first.

GEORGE:

Be back in a minute.

He crosses the stage, leaping over the puddles.

Good morning, Mother Webb.

MRS. WEBB:

Goodness! You frightened me!—Now, George, you can come in a minute out of the wet, but you know I can't ask you in.

GEORGE:

Why not—?

MRS. WEBB:

George, you know 's well as I do: the groom can't see his bride on his wedding day, not until he sees her in church.

GEORGE:

Aw!—that's just a superstition.—Good morning, Mr. Webb.

Enter MR. WEBB.

MR. WEBB:
Good morning, George.

GEORGE:
Mr. Webb, you don't believe in that superstition, do you?

MR. WEBB:
There's a lot of common sense in some superstitions, George.

He sits at the table, facing right.

MRS. WEBB:
Millions have folla'd it, George, and you don't want to be the first to fly in the face of custom.

GEORGE:
How is Emily?

MRS. WEBB:
She hasn't waked up yet. I haven't heard a sound out of her.

GEORGE:
Emily's *asleep!!!*

MRS. WEBB:
No wonder! We were up 'til all hours, sewing and packing. Now I'll tell you what I'll do; you set down here a minute with Mr. Webb and drink this cup of coffee; and I'll go upstairs and see she doesn't come down and surprise you. There's some bacon, too; but don't be long about it.

Exit MRS. WEBB.

Embarrassed silence.

MR. WEBB *dunks doughnuts in his coffee.*

More silence.

MR. WEBB:
Suddenly and loudly.

Well, George, how are you?

GEORGE:
Startled, choking over his coffee.

Oh, fine, I'm fine.

Pause.

Mr. Webb, what sense could there be in a superstition like that?

MR. WEBB:
Well, you see,—on her wedding morning a girl's head's apt to be full of . . . clothes and one thing and another. Don't you think that's probably it?

GEORGE:
Ye-e-s. I never thought of that.

MR. WEBB:
A girl's apt to be a mite nervous on her wedding day.

Pause.

GEORGE:

I wish a fellow could get married without all that marching up and down.

MR. WEBB:

Every man that's ever lived has felt that way about it, George; but it hasn't been any use. It's the womenfolk who've built up weddings, my boy. For a while now the women have it all their own. A man looks pretty small at a wedding, George. All those good women standing shoulder to shoulder making sure that the knot's tied in a mighty public way.

GEORGE:

But . . . you *believe* in it, don't you, Mr. Webb?

MR. WEBB:

With alacrity.

Oh, yes; *oh, yes.* Don't you misunderstand me, my boy. Marriage is a wonderful thing,—wonderful thing. And don't you forget that, George.

GEORGE:

No, sir.—Mr. Webb, how old were you when you got married?

MR. WEBB:

Well, you see: I'd been to college and I'd taken a little time to get settled. But Mrs. Webb—she wasn't much older than what Emily is. Oh, age hasn't much to do with it, George,—not compared with . . . uh . . . other things.

GEORGE:

What were you going to say, Mr. Webb?

MR. WEBB:
Oh, I don't know.—Was I going to say something?

Pause.

George, I was thinking the other night of some advice my father gave me when I got married. Charles, he said, Charles, start out early showing who's boss, he said. Best thing to do is to give an order, even if it don't make sense; just so she'll learn to obey. And he said: if anything about your wife irritates you—her conversation, or anything—just get up and leave the house. That'll make it clear to her, he said. And, oh, yes! he said never, *never* let your wife know how much money you have, never.

GEORGE:
Well, Mr. Webb . . . I don't think I could . . .

MR. WEBB:
So I took the opposite of my father's advice and I've been happy ever since. And let that be a lesson to you, George, never to ask advice on personal matters.—George, are you going to raise chickens on your farm?

GEORGE:
What?

MR. WEBB:
Are you going to raise chickens on your farm?

GEORGE:
Uncle Luke's never been much interested, but I thought—

MR. WEBB:
A book came into my office the other day, George, on the Philo System of raising chickens. I want you to read it. I'm thinking of

beginning in a small way in the back yard, and I'm going to put an incubator in the cellar—

Enter MRS. WEBB.

MRS. WEBB:

Charles, are you talking about that old incubator again? I thought you two'd be talking about things worth while.

MR. WEBB:

Bitingly.

Well, Myrtle, if you want to give the boy some good advice, I'll go upstairs and leave you alone with him.

MRS. WEBB:

Pulling GEORGE *up.*

George, Emily's got to come downstairs and eat her breakfast. She sends you her love but she doesn't want to lay eyes on you. Good-by.

GEORGE:

Good-by.

GEORGE *crosses the stage to his own home, bewildered and crestfallen. He slowly dodges a puddle and disappears into his house.*

MR. WEBB:

Myrtle, I guess you don't know about that older superstition.

MRS. WEBB:

What do you mean, Charles?

MR. WEBB:

Since the cave men: no bridegroom should see his father-in-law on the day of the wedding, or near it. Now remember that.

Both leave the stage.

STAGE MANAGER:

Thank you very much, Mr. and Mrs. Webb.—Now I have to interrupt again here. You see, we want to know how all this began—this wedding, this plan to spend a lifetime together. I'm awfully interested in how big things like that begin.

You know how it is: you're twenty-one or twenty-two and you make some decisions; then whisssh! you're seventy: you've been a lawyer for fifty years, and that white-haired lady at your side has eaten over fifty thousand meals with you.

How do such things begin?

George and Emily are going to show you now the conversation they had when they first knew that . . . that . . . as the saying goes . . . they were meant for one another.

But before they do it I want you to try and remember what it was like to have been very young.

And particularly the days when you were first in love; when you were like a person sleepwalking, and you didn't quite see the street you were in, and didn't quite hear everything that was said to you.

You're just a little bit crazy. Will you remember that, please?

Now they'll be coming out of high school at three o'clock. George has just been elected President of the Junior Class, and as it's June, that means he'll be President of the Senior Class all next year. And Emily's just been elected Secretary and Treasurer.

I don't have to tell you how important that is.

He places a board across the backs of two chairs, which he takes from those at the Gibbs family's table. He brings two high stools from the wings and places them behind the board. Persons sitting on the stools will be facing the audience. This is the counter of Mr. Morgan's drugstore. The sounds of young people's voices are heard off left.

Yepp,—there they are coming down Main Street now.

EMILY, *carrying an armful of—imaginary—schoolbooks, comes along Main Street from the left.*

EMILY:

I can't, Louise. I've got to go home. Good-by. Oh, Ernestine! Ernestine! Can you come over tonight and do Latin? Isn't that Cicero the worst thing—! Tell your mother you *have* to. G'by. G'by, Helen. G'by, Fred.

GEORGE, *also carrying books, catches up with her.*

GEORGE:

Can I carry your books home for you, Emily?

EMILY:

Coolly.

Why . . . uh . . . Thank you. It isn't far.

She gives them to him.

GEORGE:
Excuse me a minute, Emily.—Say, Bob, if I'm a little late, start practice anyway. And give Herb some long high ones.

EMILY:
Good-by, Lizzy.

GEORGE:
Good-by, Lizzy.—I'm awfully glad you were elected, too, Emily.

EMILY:
Thank you.

They have been standing on Main Street, almost against the back wall. They take the first steps toward the audience when GEORGE *stops and says:*

GEORGE:
Emily, why are you mad at me?

EMILY:
I'm not mad at you.

GEORGE:
You've been treating me so funny lately.

EMILY:
Well, since you ask me, I might as well say it right out, George,—

She catches sight of a teacher passing.

Good-by, Miss Corcoran.

GEORGE:
Good-by, Miss Corcoran.—Wha—what is it?

EMILY:

Not scoldingly; finding it difficult to say.

I don't like the whole change that's come over you in the last year. I'm sorry if that hurts your feelings, but I've got to—tell the truth and shame the devil.

GEORGE:

A *change?*—Wha—what do you mean?

EMILY:

Well, up to a year ago I used to like you a lot. And I used to watch you as you did everything . . . because we'd been friends so long . . . and then you began spending all your time at *baseball* . . . and you never stopped to speak to anybody any more. Not even to your own family you didn't . . . and, George, it's a fact, you've got awful conceited and stuck-up, and all the girls say so. They may not say so to your face, but that's what they say about you behind your back, and it hurts me to hear them say it, but I've got to agree with them a little. I'm sorry if it hurts your feelings . . . but I can't be sorry I said it.

GEORGE:

I . . . I'm glad you said it, Emily. I never thought that such a thing was happening to me. I guess it's hard for a fella not to have faults creep into his character.

They take a step or two in silence, then stand still in misery.

EMILY:

I always expect a man to be perfect and I think he should be.

GEORGE:

Oh . . . I don't think it's possible to be perfect, Emily.

EMILY:

Well, my *father* is, and as far as I can see *your* father is. There's no reason on earth why you shouldn't be, too.

GEORGE:

Well, I feel it's the other way round. That men aren't naturally good; but girls are.

EMILY:

Well, you might as well know right now that I'm not perfect. It's not as easy for a girl to be perfect as a man, because we girls are more—more—nervous.—Now I'm sorry I said all that about you. I don't know what made me say it.

GEORGE:

Emily,—

EMILY:

Now I can see it's not the truth at all. And I suddenly feel that it isn't important, anyway.

GEORGE:

Emily . . . would you like an ice-cream soda, or something, before you go home?

EMILY:

Well, thank you . . . I would.

They advance toward the audience and make an abrupt right turn, opening the door of Morgan's drugstore. Under strong emotion, EMILY *keeps her face down.* GEORGE *speaks to some passers-by.*

GEORGE:

Hello, Stew,—how are you?—Good afternoon, Mrs. Slocum.

The STAGE MANAGER, *wearing spectacles and assuming the role of Mr. Morgan, enters abruptly from the right and stands between the audience and the counter of his soda fountain.*

STAGE MANAGER:
Hello, George. Hello, Emily.—What'll you have?—Why, Emily Webb,—what you been crying about?

GEORGE:
He gropes for an explanation.

She . . . she just got an awful scare, Mr. Morgan. She almost got run over by that hardware-store wagon. Everybody says that Tom Huckins drives like a crazy man.

STAGE MANAGER:
Drawing a drink of water.

Well, now! You take a drink of water, Emily. You look all shook up. I tell you, you've got to look both ways before you cross Main Street these days. Gets worse every year.—What'll you have?

EMILY:
I'll have a strawberry phosphate, thank you, Mr. Morgan.

GEORGE:
No, no, Emily. Have an ice-cream soda with me. Two strawberry ice-cream sodas, Mr. Morgan.

STAGE MANAGER:
Working the faucets.

Two strawberry ice-cream sodas, yes sir. Yes, sir. There are a hundred and twenty-five horses in Grover's Corners this minute I'm talking to you. State Inspector was in here yesterday. And now they're bringing in these auto-mo-biles, the best thing to do is to just stay home. Why, I can remember when a dog could go to sleep all day in the middle of Main Street and nothing come along to disturb him.

He sets the imaginary glasses before them.

There they are. Enjoy 'em.

He sees a customer, right.

Yes, Mrs. Ellis. What can I do for you?

He goes out right.

EMILY:
They're so expensive.

GEORGE:
No, no,—don't you think of that. We're celebrating our election. And then do you know what else I'm celebrating?

EMILY:
N-no.

GEORGE:
I'm celebrating because I've got a friend who tells me all the things that ought to be told me.

EMILY:
George, *please* don't think of that. I don't know why I said it. It's not true. You're—

GEORGE:
No, Emily, you stick to it. I'm glad you spoke to me like you did.

But you'll *see:* I'm going to change so quick—you bet I'm going to change. And, Emily, I want to ask you a favor.

EMILY:
What?

GEORGE:
Emily, if I go away to State Agriculture College next year, will you write me a letter once in a while?

EMILY:
I certainly will. I certainly will, George . . .

Pause. They start sipping the sodas through the straws.

It certainly seems like being away three years you'd get out of touch with things. Maybe letters from Grover's Corners wouldn't be so interesting after a while. Grover's Corners isn't a very important place when you think of all—New Hampshire; but I think it's a very nice town.

GEORGE:
The day wouldn't come when I wouldn't want to know everything that's happening here. I know *that's* true, Emily.

EMILY:
Well, I'll try to make my letters interesting.

Pause.

GEORGE:
Y'know. Emily, whenever I meet a farmer I ask him if he thinks it's important to go to Agriculture School to be a good farmer.

EMILY:
Why, George—

GEORGE:
Yeah, and some of them say that it's even a waste of time. You can get all those things, anyway, out of the pamphlets the government sends out. And Uncle Luke's getting old,—he's about ready for me to start in taking over his farm tomorrow, if I could.

EMILY:
My!

GEORGE:
And, like you say, being gone all that time . . . in other places and meeting other people . . . Gosh, if anything like that can happen I don't want to go away. I guess new people aren't any better than old ones. I'll bet they almost never are. Emily . . . I feel that you're as good a friend as I've got. I don't need to go and meet the people in other towns.

EMILY:
But, George, maybe it's very important for you to go and learn all that about—cattle judging and soils and those things. . . . Of course, I don't know.

GEORGE:
After a pause, very seriously.

Emily, I'm going to make up my mind right now. I won't go. I'll tell Pa about it tonight.

EMILY:
Why, George, I don't see why you have to decide right now. It's a whole year away.

GEORGE:

Emily, I'm glad you spoke to me about that . . . that fault in my character. What you said was right; but there was *one* thing wrong in it, and that was when you said that for a year I wasn't noticing people, and . . . you, for instance. Why, you say you were watching me when I did everything . . . I was doing the same about you all the time. Why, sure,—I always thought about you as one of the chief people I thought about. I always made sure where you were sitting on the bleachers, and who you were with, and for three days now I've been trying to walk home with you; but something's always got in the way. Yesterday I was standing over against the wall waiting for you, and you walked home with *Miss Corcoran.*

EMILY:

George! . . . Life's awful funny! How could I have known that? Why, I thought—

GEORGE:

Listen, Emily, I'm going to tell you why I'm not going to Agriculture School. I think that once you've found a person that you're very fond of . . . I mean a person who's fond of you, too, and likes you enough to be interested in your character . . . Well, I think that's just as important as college is, and even more so. That's what I think.

EMILY:

I think it's awfully important, too.

GEORGE:

Emily.

EMILY:

Y-yes, George.

GEORGE:

Emily, if I *do* improve and make a big change . . . would you be . . . I mean: *could* you be . . .

EMILY:

I . . . I am now; I always have been.

GEORGE:

Pause.

So I guess this is an important talk we've been having.

EMILY:

Yes . . . yes.

GEORGE:

Takes a deep breath and straightens his back.

Wait just a minute and I'll walk you home.

With mounting alarm he digs into his pockets for the money.

The STAGE MANAGER *enters, right.*

GEORGE, *deeply embarrassed, but direct, says to him:*

Mr. Morgan, I'll have to go home and get the money to pay you for this. It'll only take me a minute.

STAGE MANAGER:

Pretending to be affronted.

What's that? George Gibbs, do you mean to tell me—!

GEORGE:

Yes, but I had reasons, Mr. Morgan.—Look, here's my gold watch to keep until I come back with the money.

STAGE MANAGER:

That's all right. Keep your watch. I'll trust you.

GEORGE:

I'll be back in five minutes.

STAGE MANAGER:

I'll trust you ten years, George,—not a day over.—Got all over your shock, Emily?

EMILY:

Yes, thank you, Mr. Morgan. It was nothing.

GEORGE:

Taking up the books from the counter.

I'm ready.

They walk in grave silence across the stage and pass through the trellis at the Webbs' back door and disappear.

The STAGE MANAGER *watches them go out, then turns to the audience, removing his spectacles.*

STAGE MANAGER:

Well,—

He claps his hands as a signal.

Now we're ready to get on with the wedding.

He stands waiting while the set is prepared for the next scene.

STAGEHANDS *remove the chairs, tables and trellises from the Gibbs and Webb houses.*

They arrange the pews for the church in the center of the stage. The congregation will sit facing the back wall. The aisle of the church starts at the center of the back wall and comes toward the audience.

A small platform is placed against the back wall on which the stage manager will stand later, playing the minister.

The image of a stained-glass window is cast from a lantern slide upon the back wall.

When all is ready the STAGE MANAGER *strolls to the center of the stage, down front, and, musingly, addresses the audience.*

There are a lot of things to be said about a wedding; there are a lot of thoughts that go on during a wedding.

We can't get them all into one wedding, naturally, and especially not into a wedding at Grover's Corners, where they're awfully plain and short.

In this wedding I play the minister. That gives me the right to say a few more things about it.

For a while now, the play gets pretty serious.

Y'see, some churches say that marriage is a sacrament. I don't quite know what that means, but I can guess. Like Mrs. Gibbs said a few minutes ago: People were made to live two-by-two.

This is a good wedding, but people are so put together that even at a good wedding there's a lot of confusion way down deep in people's minds and we thought that that ought to be in our play, too.

The real hero of this scene isn't on the stage at all, and you know who that is. It's like what one of those European fellas said: Every child born into the world is nature's attempt to make a perfect human being. Well, we've seen nature pushing and contriving for some time now. We all know that nature's interested in quantity; but I think she's interested in quality, too,—that's why I'm in the ministry.

And don't forget all the other witnesses at this wedding,—the ancestors. Millions of them. Most of them set out to live two-by-two, also. Millions of them.

Well, that's all my sermon. 'Twan't very long, anyway.

The organ starts playing Handel's "Largo."

The congregation streams into the church and sits in silence.

Church bells are heard.

MRS. GIBBS *sits in the front row, the first seat on the aisle, the right section; next to her are* REBECCA *and* DR. GIBBS.

Across the aisle MRS. WEBB, WALLY *and* MR. WEBB. *A small choir takes its place, facing the audience under the stained-glass window.*

MRS. WEBB, *on the way to her place, turns back and speaks to the audience.*

MRS. WEBB:

I don't know why on earth I should be crying. I suppose there's nothing to cry about. It came over me at breakfast this morning; there was Emily eating her breakfast as she's done for seventeen years and now she's going off to eat it in someone else's house. I suppose that's it.

And Emily! She suddenly said: I can't eat another mouthful, and she put her head down on the table and *she* cried.

She starts toward her seat in the church, but turns back and adds:

Oh, I've got to say it: you know, there's something downright cruel about sending our girls out into marriage this way. I hope some of her girl friends have told her a thing or two. It's cruel, I know, but I couldn't bring myself to say anything. I went into it blind as a bat myself.

In half-amused exasperation.

The whole world's wrong, that's what's the matter.

There they come.

She hurries to her place in the pew.

GEORGE *starts to come down the right aisle of the theatre, through the audience.*

Suddenly THREE MEMBERS *of his baseball team appear by the right proscenium pillar and start whistling and catcalling to him. They are dressed for the ball field.*

THE BASEBALL PLAYERS:
Eh, George, George! Hast—yaow! Look at him, fellas—he looks scared to death. Yaow! George, don't look so innocent, you old geezer. We know what you're thinking. Don't disgrace the team, big boy. Whoo-oo-oo.

STAGE MANAGER:
All right! All right! That'll do. That's enough of that.

Smiling, he pushes them off the stage. They lean back to shout a few more catcalls.

There used to be an awful lot of that kind of thing at weddings in the old days,—Rome, and later. We're more civilized now,—so they say.

The choir starts singing "Love Divine, All Love Excelling—." GEORGE *has reached the stage. He stares at the congregation a moment, then takes a few steps of withdrawal, toward the right proscenium pillar. His mother, from the front row, seems to have felt his confusion. She leaves her seat and comes down the aisle quickly to him.*

MRS. GIBBS:
George! George! What's the matter?

GEORGE:
Ma, I don't want to grow old. Why's everybody pushing me so?

MRS. GIBBS:
Why, George . . . you wanted it.

GEORGE:
No, Ma, listen to me—

MRS. GIBBS:

No, no, George,—you're a man now.

GEORGE:

Listen, Ma,—for the last time I ask you . . . All I want to do is to be a fella—

MRS. GIBBS:

George! If anyone should hear you! Now stop. Why, I'm ashamed of you!

GEORGE:

He comes to himself and looks over the scene.

What? Where's Emily?

MRS. GIBBS:

Relieved.

George! You gave me such a turn.

GEORGE:

Cheer up, Ma. I'm getting married.

MRS. GIBBS:

Let me catch my breath a minute.

GEORGE:

Comforting her.

Now, Ma, you save Thursday nights. Emily and I are coming over to dinner every Thursday night . . . you'll see. Ma, what are you crying for? Come on; we've got to get ready for this.

MRS. GIBBS, *mastering her emotion, fixes his tie and whispers to him.*

In the meantime, EMILY, *in white and wearing her wedding veil, has come through the audience and mounted onto the stage. She too draws back, frightened, when she sees the congregation in the church. The choir begins: "Blessed Be the Tie That Binds."*

EMILY:

I never felt so alone in my whole life. And George over there, looking so . . . ! I *hate* him. I wish I were dead. Papa! Papa!

MR. WEBB:

Leaves his seat in the pews and comes toward her anxiously.

Emily! Emily! Now don't get upset. . . .

EMILY:

But, Papa,—I don't want to get married. . . .

MR. WEBB:

Sh—sh—Emily. Everything's all right.

EMILY:

Why can't I stay for a while just as I am? Let's go away,—

MR. WEBB:

No, no, Emily. Now stop and think a minute.

EMILY:

Don't you remember that you used to say,—all the time you used to say—all the time: that I was *your* girl! There must be lots of places we can go to. I'll work for you. I could keep house.

MR. WEBB:
Sh . . . You mustn't think of such things. You're just nervous, Emily.

He turns and calls:

George! George! Will you come here a minute?

He leads her toward George.

Why you're marrying the best young fellow in the world. George is a fine fellow.

EMILY:
But Papa,—

MRS. GIBBS *returns unobtrusively to her seat.*

MR. WEBB *has one arm around his daughter. He places his hand on* GEORGE'S *shoulder.*

MR. WEBB:
I'm giving away my daughter, George. Do you think you can take care of her?

GEORGE:
Mr. Webb, I want to . . . I want to try. Emily, I'm going to do my best. I love you, Emily. I need you.

EMILY:
Well, if you love me, help me. All I want is someone to love me.

GEORGE:
I will, Emily. Emily, I'll try.

EMILY:

And I mean for *ever.* Do you hear? For ever and ever.

They fall into each other's arms.

The March from Lohengrin *is heard.*

The STAGE MANAGER, *as* CLERGYMAN, *stands on the box, up center.*

MR. WEBB:

Come, they're waiting for us. Now you know it'll be all right. Come, quick.

GEORGE *slips away and takes his place beside the* STAGE MANAGER-CLERGYMAN.

EMILY *proceeds up the aisle on her father's arm.*

STAGE MANAGER:

Do you, George, take this woman, Emily, to be your wedded wife, to have . . .

MRS. SOAMES *has been sitting in the last row of the congregation.*

She now turns to her neighbors and speaks in a shrill voice. Her chatter drowns out the rest of the clergyman's words.

MRS. SOAMES:

Perfectly lovely wedding! Loveliest wedding I ever saw. Oh, I do love a good wedding, don't you? Doesn't she make a lovely bride?

GEORGE:

I do.

STAGE MANAGER:

Do you, Emily, take this man, George, to be your wedded husband,—

Again his further words are covered by those of MRS. SOAMES.

MRS. SOAMES:

Don't know *when* I've seen such a lovely wedding. But I always cry. Don't know why it is, but I always cry. I just like to see young people happy, don't you? Oh, I think it's lovely.

The ring.

The kiss.

The stage is suddenly arrested into silent tableau.

The STAGE MANAGER, *his eyes on the distance, as though to himself:*

STAGE MANAGER:

I've married over two hundred couples in my day.

Do I believe in it?

I don't know.

M. . . . marries N. . . . millions of them.

The cottage, the go-cart, the Sunday-afternoon drives in the Ford, the first rheumatism, the grandchildren, the second rheumatism, the deathbed, the reading of the will,—

He now looks at the audience for the first time, with a warm smile that removes any sense of cynicism from the next line.

Once in a thousand times it's interesting.

—Well, let's have Mendelssohn's "Wedding March"!

The organ picks up the March.

The BRIDE *and* GROOM *come down the aisle, radiant, but trying to be very dignified.*

MRS. SOAMES:

Aren't they a lovely couple? Oh, I've never been to such a nice wedding. I'm sure they'll be happy. I always say: *happiness,* that's the great thing! The important thing is to be happy.

The BRIDE *and* GROOM *reach the steps leading into the audience. A bright light is thrown upon them. They descend into the auditorium and run up the aisle joyously.*

STAGE MANAGER:

That's all the Second Act, folks. Ten minutes' intermission.

CURTAIN

Act III

During the intermission the audience has seen the stagehands arranging the stage. On the right-hand side, a little right of the center, ten or twelve ordinary chairs have been placed in three openly spaced rows facing the audience.

These are graves in the cemetery.

Toward the end of the intermission the actors enter and take their places. The front row contains: toward the center of the stage, an empty chair; then MRS. GIBBS*;* SIMON STIMSON.

The second row contains, among others, MRS. SOAMES.

The third row has WALLY WEBB.

The dead do not turn their heads or their eyes to right or left, but they sit in a quiet without stiffness. When they speak their tone is matter-of-fact, without sentimentality and, above all, without lugubriousness.

The STAGE MANAGER *takes his accustomed place and waits for the house lights to go down.*

STAGE MANAGER:

This time nine years have gone by, friends—summer, 1913.

Gradual changes in Grover's Corners. Horses are getting rarer.

Farmers coming into town in Fords.

Everybody locks their house doors now at night. Ain't been any burglars in town yet, but everybody's heard about 'em.

You'd be surprised, though—on the whole, things don't change much around here.

This is certainly an important part of Grover's Corners. It's on a hilltop—a windy hilltop—lots of sky, lots of clouds,—often lots of sun and moon and stars.

You come up here, on a fine afternoon and you can see range on range of hills—awful blue they are—up there by Lake Sunapee and Lake Winnipesaukee . . . and way up, if you've got a glass, you can see the White Mountains and Mt. Washington—where North Conway and Conway is. And, of course, our favorite mountain, Mt. Monadnock, 's right here—and all these towns that lie around it: Jaffrey, 'n East Jaffrey, 'n Peterborough, 'n Dublin; and

Then pointing down in the audience.

there, quite a ways down, is Grover's Corners.

Yes, beautiful spot up here. Mountain laurel and li-lacks. I often wonder why people like to be buried in Woodlawn and Brooklyn when they might pass the same time up here in New Hampshire.

Over there—

Pointing to stage left.

are the old stones,—1670, 1680. Strong-minded people that come a long way to be independent. Summer people walk around there laughing at the funny words on the tombstones . . . it don't do any harm. And genealogists come up from Boston—get paid by city people for looking up their ancestors. They want to make sure they're Daughters of the American Revolution and of the *Mayflower*. . . . Well, I guess that don't do any harm, either.

Wherever you come near the human race, there's layers and layers of nonsense. . . .

Over there are some Civil War veterans. Iron flags on their graves . . . New Hampshire boys . . . had a notion that the Union ought to be kept together, though they'd never seen more than fifty miles of it themselves. All they knew was the name, friends—the United States of America. The United States of America. And they went and died about it.

This here is the new part of the cemetery. Here's your friend Mrs. Gibbs. 'N let me see—Here's Mr. Stimson, organist at the Congregational Church. And Mrs. Soames who enjoyed the wedding so—you remember? Oh, and a lot of others. And Editor Webb's boy, Wallace, whose appendix burst while he was on a Boy Scout trip to Crawford Notch.

Yes, an awful lot of sorrow has sort of quieted down up here.

People just wild with grief have brought their relatives up to this hill. We all know how it is . . . and then time . . . and sunny days . . . and rainy days . . .'n snow . . . We're all glad they're in a beautiful place and we're coming up here ourselves when our fit's over.

Now there are some things we all know, but we don't take'm out and look at'm very often. We all know that *something* is eternal. And it ain't houses and it ain't names, and it ain't earth, and it ain't even the stars . . . everybody knows in their bones that *something* is eternal, and that something has to do with human beings. All the greatest people ever lived have been telling us that for five thousand years and yet you'd be surprised how people are always losing hold of it. There's something way down deep that's eternal about every human being.

Pause.

You know as well as I do that the dead don't stay interested in us living people for very long. Gradually, gradually, they lose hold of the earth . . . and the ambitions they had . . . and the pleasures they had . . . and the things they suffered . . . and the people they loved.

They get weaned away from earth—that's the way I put it,—weaned away.

And they stay here while the earth part of 'em burns away, burns out; and all that time they slowly get indifferent to what's goin' on in Grover's Corners.

They're waitin'. They're waitin' for something that they feel is comin'. Something important, and great. Aren't they waitin' for the eternal part in them to come out clear?

Some of the things they're going to say maybe'll hurt your feelings—but that's the way it is: mother 'n daughter . . . husband 'n wife . . . enemy 'n enemy . . . money 'n miser . . . all those terribly important things kind of grow pale around here. And what's left when memory's gone, and your identity, Mrs. Smith?

He looks at the audience a minute, then turns to the stage.

Well! There are some *living* people. There's Joe Stoddard, our undertaker, supervising a new-made grave. And here comes a Grover's Corners boy, that left town to go out West.

JOE STODDARD *has hovered about in the background.* SAM CRAIG *enters left, wiping his forehead from the exertion. He carries an umbrella and strolls front.*

SAM CRAIG:

Good afternoon, Joe Stoddard.

JOE STODDARD:

Good afternoon, good afternoon. Let me see now: do I know you?

SAM CRAIG:

I'm Sam Craig.

JOE STODDARD:

Gracious sakes' alive! Of all people! I should'a knowed you'd be back for the funeral. You've been away a long time, Sam.

SAM CRAIG:

Yes, I've been away over twelve years. I'm in business out in Buffalo now, Joe. But I was in the East when I got news of my cousin's death, so I thought I'd combine things a little and come and see the old home. You look well.

JOE STODDARD:

Yes, yes, can't complain. Very sad, our journey today, Samuel.

SAM CRAIG:

Yes.

JOE STODDARD:

Yes, yes. I always say I hate to supervise when a young person is taken. They'll be here in a few minutes now. I had to come here early today—my son's supervisin' at the home.

SAM CRAIG:

Reading stones.

Old Farmer McCarty, I used to do chores for him—after school. He had the lumbago.

JOE STODDARD:

Yes, we brought Farmer McCarty here a number of years ago now.

SAM CRAIG:

Staring at Mrs. Gibbs' knees.

Why, this is my Aunt Julia . . . I'd forgotten that she'd . . . of course, of course.

JOE STODDARD:

Yes, Doc Gibbs lost his wife two-three years ago . . . about this time. And today's another pretty bad blow for him, too.

MRS. GIBBS:

To Simon Stimson: in an even voice.

That's my sister Carey's boy, Sam . . . Sam Craig.

SIMON STIMSON:

I'm always uncomfortable when *they're* around.

MRS. GIBBS:

Simon.

SAM CRAIG:

Do they choose their own verses much, Joe?

JOE STODDARD:

No . . . not usual. Mostly the bereaved pick a verse.

SAM CRAIG:

Doesn't sound like Aunt Julia. There aren't many of those Hersey sisters left now. Let me see: where are . . . I wanted to look at my father's and mother's . . .

JOE STODDARD:

Over there with the Craigs . . . Avenue F.

SAM CRAIG:

Reading Simon Stimson's epitaph.

He was organist at church, wasn't he?—Hm, drank a lot, we used to say.

JOE STODDARD:

Nobody was supposed to know about it. He'd seen a peck of trouble.

Behind his hand.

Took his own life, y' know?

SAM CRAIG:

Oh, did he?

JOE STODDARD:

Hung himself in the attic. They tried to hush it up, but of course it got around. He chose his own epy-taph. You can see it there. It ain't a verse exactly.

SAM CRAIG:

Why, it's just some notes of music—what is it?

JOE STODDARD:

Oh, I wouldn't know. It was wrote up in the Boston papers at the time.

SAM CRAIG:

Joe, what did she die of?

JOE STODDARD:

Who?

SAM CRAIG:

My cousin.

JOE STODDARD:

Oh, didn't you know? Had some trouble bringing a baby into the world. 'Twas her second, though. There's a little boy 'bout four years old.

SAM CRAIG:

Opening his umbrella.

The grave's going to be over there?

JOE STODDARD:

Yes, there ain't much more room over here among the Gibbses, so they're opening up a whole new Gibbs section over by Avenue B. You'll excuse me now. I see they're comin'.

From left to center, at the back of the stage, comes a procession. FOUR MEN *carry a casket, invisible to us. All the rest are under umbrellas. One can vaguely see:* DR. GIBBS, GEORGE, THE WEBBS, *etc. They gather about a grave in the back center of the stage, a little to the left of center.*

MRS. SOAMES:

Who is it, Julia?

MRS. GIBBS:

Without raising her eyes.

My daughter-in-law, Emily Webb.

MRS. SOAMES:
A little surprised, but no emotion.

Well, I declare! The road up here must have been awful muddy. What did she die of, Julia?

MRS. GIBBS:
In childbirth.

MRS. SOAMES:
Childbirth.

Almost with a laugh.

I'd forgotten all about that. My, wasn't life awful—

With a sigh.

and wonderful.

SIMON STIMSON:
With a sideways glance.

Wonderful, was it?

MRS. GIBBS:
Simon! Now, remember!

MRS. SOAMES:
I remember Emily's wedding. Wasn't it a lovely wedding! And I remember her reading the class poem at Graduation Exercises. Emily was one of the brightest girls ever graduated from High School. I've heard Principal Wilkins say so time after time. I called on them at their new farm, just before I died. Perfectly beautiful farm.

A WOMAN FROM AMONG THE DEAD:
It's on the same road we lived on.

A MAN AMONG THE DEAD:
Yepp, right smart farm.

They subside. The group by the grave starts singing "Blessed Be the Tie That Binds."

A WOMAN AMONG THE DEAD:
I always liked that hymn. I was hopin' they'd sing a hymn.

Pause. Suddenly EMILY *appears from among the umbrellas. She is wearing a white dress. Her hair is down her back and tied by a white ribbon like a little girl. She comes slowly, gazing wonderingly at the dead, a little dazed.*

She stops halfway and smiles faintly. After looking at the mourners for a moment, she walks slowly to the vacant chair beside Mrs. Gibbs and sits down.

EMILY:
To them all, quietly, smiling.

Hello.

MRS. SOAMES:
Hello, Emily.

A MAN AMONG THE DEAD:
Hello, M's Gibbs.

EMILY:
Warmly.

Hello, Mother Gibbs.

MRS. GIBBS:
Emily.

EMILY:
Hello.

With surprise.

It's raining.

Her eyes drift back to the funeral company.

MRS. GIBBS:
Yes . . . They'll be gone soon, dear. Just rest yourself.

EMILY:
It seems thousands and thousands of years since I . . . Papa remembered that that was my favorite hymn.

Oh, I wish I'd been here a long time. I don't like being new here.—How do you do, Mr. Stimson?

SIMON STIMSON:
How do you do, Emily.

EMILY *continues to look about her with a wondering smile; as though to shut out from her mind the thought of the funeral company she starts speaking to Mrs. Gibbs with a touch of nervousness.*

EMILY:

Mother Gibbs, George and I have made that farm into just the best place you ever saw. We thought of you all the time. We wanted to show you the new barn and a great long ce-ment drinking fountain for the stock. We bought that out of the money you left us.

MRS. GIBBS:

I did?

EMILY:

Don't you remember, Mother Gibbs—the legacy you left us? Why, it was over three hundred and fifty dollars.

MRS. GIBBS:

Yes, yes, Emily.

EMILY:

Well, there's a patent device on the drinking fountain so that it never overflows, Mother Gibbs, and it never sinks below a certain mark they have there. It's fine.

Her voice trails off and her eyes return to the funeral group.

It won't be the same to George without me, but it's a lovely farm.

Suddenly she looks directly at Mrs. Gibbs.

Live people don't understand, do they?

MRS. GIBBS:

No, dear—not very much.

EMILY:

They're sort of shut up in little boxes, aren't they? I feel as though I knew them last a thousand years ago . . . My boy is spending the day at Mrs. Carter's.

She sees MR. CARTER *among the dead.*

Oh, Mr. Carter, my little boy is spending the day at your house.

MR. CARTER:

Is he?

EMILY:

Yes, he loves it there.—Mother Gibbs, we have a Ford, too. Never gives any trouble. I don't drive, though. Mother Gibbs, when does this feeling go away?—Of being . . . one of *them*? How long does it . . . ?

MRS. GIBBS:

Sh! dear. Just wait and be patient.

EMILY:

With a sigh.

I know.—Look, they're finished. They're going.

MRS. GIBBS:

Sh—.

The umbrellas leave the stage. DR. GIBBS *has come over to his wife's grave and stands before it a moment.* EMILY *looks up at his face.* MRS. GIBBS *does not raise her eyes.*

EMILY:

Look! Father Gibbs is bringing some of my flowers to you. He looks just like George, doesn't he? Oh, Mother Gibbs, I never realized before how troubled and how . . . how in the dark live persons are. Look at him. I loved him so. From morning till night, that's all they are—troubled.

DR. GIBBS *goes off.*

THE DEAD:

Little cooler than it was.—Yes, that rain's cooled it off a little. Those northeast winds always do the same thing, don't they? If it isn't a rain, it's a three-day blow.—

A patient calm falls on the stage. The STAGE MANAGER *appears at his proscenium pillar, smoking.* EMILY *sits up abruptly with an idea.*

EMILY:

But, Mother Gibbs, one can go back; one can go back there again . . . into living. I feel it. I know it. Why just then for a moment I was thinking about . . . about the farm . . . and for a minute I *was* there, and my baby was on my lap as plain as day.

MRS. GIBBS:

Yes, of course you can.

EMILY:

I can go back there and live all those days over again . . . why not?

MRS. GIBBS:

All I can say is, Emily, don't.

EMILY:

She appeals urgently to the stage manager.

But it's true, isn't it? I can go and live . . . back there . . . again.

STAGE MANAGER:
Yes, some have tried—but they soon come back here.

MRS. GIBBS:
Don't do it, Emily.

MRS. SOAMES:
Emily, don't. It's not what you think it'd be.

EMILY:
But I won't live over a sad day. I'll choose a happy one—I'll choose the day I first knew that I loved George. Why should that be painful?

They are silent. Her question turns to the stage manager.

STAGE MANAGER:
You not only live it; but you watch yourself living it.

EMILY:
Yes?

STAGE MANAGER:
And as you watch it, you see the thing that they—down there—never know. You see the future. You know what's going to happen afterwards.

EMILY:
But is that—painful? Why?

MRS. GIBBS:

That's not the only reason why you shouldn't do it, Emily. When you've been here longer you'll see that our life here is to forget all that, and think only of what's ahead, and be ready for what's ahead. When you've been here longer you'll understand.

EMILY:

Softly.

But, Mother Gibbs, how can I *ever* forget that life? It's all I know. It's all I had.

MRS. SOAMES:

Oh, Emily. It isn't wise. Really, it isn't.

EMILY:

But it's a thing I must know for myself. I'll choose a happy day, anyway.

MRS. GIBBS:

No!—At least, choose an unimportant day. Choose the least important day in your life. It will be important enough.

EMILY:

To herself.

Then it can't be since I was married; or since the baby was born.

To the stage manager, eagerly.

I can choose a birthday at least, can't I?—I choose my twelfth birthday.

STAGE MANAGER:

All right. February 11th, 1899. A Tuesday.—Do you want any special time of day?

EMILY:

Oh, I want the whole day.

STAGE MANAGER:

We'll begin at dawn. You remember it had been snowing for several days; but it had stopped the night before, and they had begun clearing the roads. The sun's coming up.

EMILY:

With a cry; rising.

There's Main Street . . . why, that's Mr. Morgan's drugstore before he changed it! . . . And there's the livery stable.

The stage at no time in this act has been very dark; but now the left half of the stage gradually becomes very bright—the brightness of a crisp winter morning. EMILY *walks toward Main Street.*

STAGE MANAGER:

Yes, it's 1899. This is fourteen years ago.

EMILY:

Oh, that's the town I knew as a little girl. And, *look,* there's the old white fence that used to be around our house. Oh, I'd forgotten that! Oh, I love it so! Are they inside?

STAGE MANAGER:

Yes, your mother'll be coming downstairs in a minute to make breakfast.

EMILY:

Softly.

Will she?

STAGE MANAGER:

And you remember: your father had been away for several days; he came back on the early-morning train.

EMILY:

No . . . ?

STAGE MANAGER:

He'd been back to his college to make a speech—in western New York, at Clinton.

EMILY:

Look! There's Howie Newsome. There's our policeman. But he's *dead;* he *died.*

The voices of HOWIE NEWSOME, CONSTABLE WARREN *and* JOE CROWELL, JR., *are heard at the left of the stage.* EMILY *listens in delight.*

HOWIE NEWSOME:

Whoa, Bessie!—Bessie! 'Morning, Bill.

CONSTABLE WARREN:

Morning, Howie.

HOWIE NEWSOME:

You're up early.

CONSTABLE WARREN:

Been rescuin' a party; darn near froze to death, down by Polish Town thar. Got drunk and lay out in the snowdrifts. Thought he was in bed when I shook'm.

EMILY:

Why, there's Joe Crowell. . . .

JOE CROWELL:

Good morning, Mr. Warren. 'Morning, Howie.

MRS. WEBB *has appeared in her kitchen, but* EMILY *does not see her until she calls.*

MRS. WEBB:

Chil-*dren!* Wally! Emily! . . . Time to get up.

EMILY:

Mama, I'm here! Oh! how young Mama looks! I didn't know Mama was ever that young.

MRS. WEBB:

You can come and dress by the kitchen fire, if you like; but hurry.

HOWIE NEWSOME *has entered along Main Street and brings the milk to Mrs. Webb's door.*

Good morning, Mr. Newsome. Whhhh—it's cold.

HOWIE NEWSOME:

Ten below by my barn, Mrs. Webb.

MRS. WEBB:

Think of it! Keep yourself wrapped up.

She takes her bottles in, shuddering.

EMILY:

With an effort.

Mama, I can't find my blue hair ribbon anywhere.

MRS. WEBB:

Just open your eyes, dear, that's all. I laid it out for you special—on the dresser, there. If it were a snake it would bite you.

EMILY:

Yes, yes . . .

She puts her hand on her heart. MR. WEBB *comes along Main Street, where he meets* CONSTABLE WARREN. *Their movements and voices are increasingly lively in the sharp air.*

MR. WEBB:

Good morning, Bill.

CONSTABLE WARREN:

Good morning, Mr. Webb. You're up early.

MR. WEBB:

Yes, just been back to my old college in New York State. Been any trouble here?

CONSTABLE WARREN:

Well, I was called up this mornin' to rescue a Polish fella—darn near froze to death he was.

MR. WEBB:

We must get it in the paper.

CONSTABLE WARREN:

'Twan't much.

EMILY:

Whispers.

Papa.

MR. WEBB *shakes the snow off his feet and enters his house.* CONSTABLE WARREN *goes off, right.*

MR. WEBB:

Good morning, Mother.

MRS. WEBB:

How did it go, Charles?

MR. WEBB:

Oh, fine, I guess. I told'm a few things.—Everything all right here?

MRS. WEBB:

Yes—can't think of anything that's happened, special. Been right cold. Howie Newsome says it's ten below over to his barn.

MR. WEBB:

Yes, well, it's colder than that at Hamilton College. Students' ears are falling off. It ain't Christian.—Paper have any mistakes in it?

MRS. WEBB:

None that I noticed. Coffee's ready when you want it.

He starts upstairs.

Charles! Don't forget, it's Emily's birthday. Did you remember to get her something?

MR. WEBB:

Patting his pocket.

Yes, I've got something here.

Calling up the stairs.

Where's my girl? Where's my birthday girl?

He goes off left.

MRS. WEBB:

Don't interrupt her now, Charles. You can see her at breakfast. She's slow enough as it is. Hurry up, children! It's seven o'clock. Now, I don't want to call you again.

EMILY:

Softly, more in wonder than in grief.

I can't bear it. They're so young and beautiful. Why did they ever have to get old? Mama, I'm here. I'm grown up. I love you all, everything.—I can't look at everything hard enough.

She looks questioningly at the stage manager, saying or suggesting: "Can I go in?" He nods briefly. She crosses to the inner door to the kitchen, left of her mother, and as though entering the room, says, suggesting the voice of a girl of twelve:

Good morning, Mama.

MRS. WEBB:

Crossing to embrace and kiss her; in her characteristic matter-of-fact manner.

Well, now, dear, a very happy birthday to my girl and many happy returns. There are some surprises waiting for you on the kitchen table.

EMILY:

Oh, Mama, you *shouldn't* have.

She throws an anguished glance at the stage manager.

I can't—I can't.

MRS. WEBB:

Facing the audience, over her stove.

But birthday or no birthday, I want you to eat your breakfast good and slow. I want you to grow up and be a good strong girl.

That in the blue paper is from your Aunt Carrie; and I reckon you can guess who brought the post-card album. I found it on the doorstep when I brought in the milk—George Gibbs . . . must have come over in the cold pretty early . . . right nice of him.

EMILY:

To herself.

Oh, George! I'd forgotten that. . . .

MRS. WEBB:

Chew that bacon good and slow. It'll help keep you warm on a cold day.

EMILY:

With mounting urgency.

Oh, Mama, just look at me one minute as though you really saw me. Mama, fourteen years have gone by. I'm dead. You're a grandmother, Mama. I married George Gibbs, Mama. Wally's dead, too. Mama, his appendix burst on a camping trip to North Conway. We felt just terrible about it—don't you remember? But, just for a moment now we're all together. Mama, just for a moment we're happy. *Let's look at one another.*

MRS. WEBB:

That in the yellow paper is something I found in the attic among your grandmother's things. You're old enough to wear it now, and I thought you'd like it.

EMILY:

And this is from you. Why, Mama, it's just lovely and it's just what I wanted. It's beautiful!

She flings her arms around her mother's neck. Her MOTHER *goes on with her cooking, but is pleased.*

MRS. WEBB:

Well, I hoped you'd like it. Hunted all over. Your Aunt Norah couldn't find one in Concord, so I had to send all the way to Boston.

Laughing.

Wally has something for you, too. He made it at manual-training class and he's very proud of it. Be sure you make a big fuss about it.—Your father has a surprise for you, too; don't know what it is myself. Sh—here he comes.

MR. WEBB:

Off stage.

Where's my girl? Where's my birthday girl?

EMILY:

In a loud voice to the stage manager.

I can't. I can't go on. It goes so fast. We don't have time to look at one another.

She breaks down sobbing.

The lights dim on the left half of the stage. MRS. WEBB *disappears.*

I didn't realize. So all that was going on and we never noticed. Take me back—up the hill—to my grave. But first: Wait! One more look.

Good-by, Good-by, world. Good-by, Grover's Corners . . . Mama and Papa. Good-by to clocks ticking . . . and Mama's sunflowers. And food and coffee. And new-ironed dresses and hot baths . . . and sleeping and waking up. Oh, Earth, you're too wonderful for anybody to realize you.

She looks toward the stage manager and asks abruptly, through her tears:

Do any human beings ever realize life while they live it?—every, every minute?

STAGE MANAGER:
No.

Pause.

The saints and poets, maybe—they do some.

EMILY:
I'm ready to go back.

She returns to her chair beside Mrs. Gibbs.

Pause.

MRS. GIBBS:
Were you happy?

EMILY:
No . . . I should have listened to you. That's all human beings are! Just blind people.

MRS. GIBBS:
Look, it's clearing up. The stars are coming out.

EMILY:
Oh, Mr. Stimson, I should have listened to them.

SIMON STIMSON:
With mounting violence; bitingly.

Yes, now you know. Now you know! That's what it was to be alive. To move about in a cloud of ignorance; to go up and down trampling on the feelings of those . . . of those about you. To spend and waste time as though you had a million years. To be always at the mercy of one self-centered passion, or another. Now you know—that's the happy existence you wanted to go back to. Ignorance and blindness.

MRS. GIBBS:
Spiritedly.

Simon Stimson, that ain't the whole truth and you know it. Emily, look at that star. I forget its name.

A MAN AMONG THE DEAD:
My boy Joel was a sailor,—knew 'em all. He'd set on the porch evenings and tell 'em all by name. Yes, sir, wonderful!

ANOTHER MAN AMONG THE DEAD:
A star's mighty good company.

A WOMAN AMONG THE DEAD:
Yes. Yes, 'tis.

SIMON STIMSON:
Here's one of *them* coming.

THE DEAD:
That's funny. 'Tain't no time for one of them to be here.—Goodness sakes.

EMILY:

Mother Gibbs, it's George.

MRS. GIBBS:

Sh, dear. Just rest yourself.

EMILY:

It's George.

GEORGE *enters from the left, and slowly comes toward them.*

A MAN FROM AMONG THE DEAD:

And my boy, Joel, who knew the stars—he used to say it took millions of years for that speck o' light to git to the earth. Don't seem like a body could believe it, but that's what he used to say—millions of years.

GEORGE *sinks to his knees then falls full length at Emily's feet.*

A WOMAN AMONG THE DEAD:

Goodness! That ain't no way to behave!

MRS. SOAMES:

He ought to be home.

EMILY:

Mother Gibbs?

MRS. GIBBS:

Yes, Emily?

EMILY:

They don't understand, do they?

MRS. GIBBS:
No, dear. They don't understand.

The STAGE MANAGER *appears at the right, one hand on a dark curtain which he slowly draws across the scene.*

In the distance a clock is heard striking the hour very faintly.

STAGE MANAGER:
Most everybody's asleep in Grover's Corners. There are a few lights on: Shorty Hawkins, down at the depot, has just watched the Albany train go by. And at the livery stable somebody's setting up late and talking.—Yes, it's clearing up. There are the stars—doing their old, old crisscross journeys in the sky. Scholars haven't settled the matter yet, but they seem to think there are no living beings up there. Just chalk . . . or fire. Only this one is straining away, straining away all the time to make something of itself. The strain's so bad that every sixteen hours everybody lies down and gets a rest.

He winds his watch.

Hm. . . . Eleven o'clock in Grover's Corners.—You get a good rest, too. Good night.

THE END

The Long Christmas Dinner

Characters

Lucia, Roderick's wife
Roderick, Mother Bayard's son
Mother Bayard
Cousin Brandon
Charles, Lucia and Roderick's son
Genevieve, Lucia and Roderick's daughter
Leonora Banning, Charles's wife
Lucia, Leonora and Charles's daughter, Samuel's twin
Samuel, Leonora and Charles's son, Lucia's twin
Roderick, Leonora and Charles's youngest son
Cousin Ermengarde
Servants
Nurses

The Scene

The dining room of the Bayard home. A long dining table is handsomely spread for Christmas dinner. The carver's place with a great turkey before it is at the right. Down left, by the proscenium arch, is a strange portal trimmed with garlands of fruits and flowers. Directly opposite, down right, is another portal hung with black velvet. The portals denote birth and death, respectively.

Along the rear wall, at the right, is a sideboard, in the center a fireplace with perhaps a portrait of a man above it, and on the left a large door into the hall.

At the table there is a chair at each end, and three chairs against the walls. The chair at the head of the table should be high-backed and with arms.

Notes for the Producer

Ninety years are traversed in this play which represents in accelerated motion ninety Christmas dinners in the Bayard household. Although the speech, the manner and business of the actors is colloquial and realistic, the production should stimulate the imagination and be implied and suggestive. Accordingly gray curtains with set pieces are recommended for the walls of the room rather than conventional scenery. In the center of the table is a bowl of Christmas greens and at the left end a wine decanter and glasses. Except for these all properties in the play are imaginary. Throughout the play the characters continue eating invisible food with imaginary knives and forks. The actors are dressed in inconspicuous clothes and must indicate their gradual increase in years through their acting.

The ladies may have shawls concealed which they gradually draw up about their shoulders as they grow older.

At the rise of the curtain the stage should be dark, gradually a bright light dims on and covers the table. Floods of light also are directed on the stage from the two portals. The flood from stage Right should be a "cool" color, and the one from stage Left "warm." If possible all lights should be kept off the walls of the room. (It may be possible, when this play is given by itself, to dispense with the curtain, so that the audience arriving will see the stage set and the table laid, though in indistinct darkness.)

Experience has shown that many companies have fallen into the practice of playing this play in a weird, lugubrious manner. Care should be taken that the conversation is normal and that after the "deaths" the play should pick up its tempo at once.

(There is no curtain. The audience arriving at the theatre sees the stage set and the table laid, though still in partial darkness. Gradually the lights in the auditorium become dim and the stage brightens until sparkling winter sunlight streams through the dining-room windows. Enter LUCIA *from the hall. She inspects the table, touching here a knife and there a fork. She talks to a servant girl who is invisible to us.)*

LUCIA. I reckon we're ready now, Gertrude. We won't ring the chimes today. I'll just call them myself. *(She goes into the hall and calls)* Roderick. Mother Bayard. We're all ready. Come to dinner.

(Enter RODERICK *pushing* MOTHER BAYARD *in a wheelchair)*

MOTHER BAYARD. . . . and a new horse too, Roderick. I used to think that only the wicked owned two horses. A new horse and a new house and a new wife!

LUCIA. Here, Mother Bayard, you sit between us.

RODERICK. Well, Mother, how do you like it? Our first Christmas dinner in the new house, hey?

MOTHER BAYARD. Tz-Tz-Tz! I don't know what your dear father would say!

*(*RODERICK *says grace)*

My dear Lucia, I can remember when there were still Indians on this very ground, and I wasn't a young girl either. I can remember when we had to cross the Mississippi on a new-made raft. I can remember when Saint Louis and Kansas City were full of Indians.

LUCIA. *(Tying a napkin around* MOTHER BAYARD*'s neck)* Imagine that! There! What a wonderful day for our first Christmas dinner: a beautiful sunny morning, snow, a splendid sermon. Dr. McCarthy preaches a splendid sermon. I cried and cried.

RODERICK. *(Extending an imaginary carving fork)* Come now, what'll you have, Mother? A little sliver of white?

LUCIA. Every last twig is wrapped around with ice. You almost never see that. Can I cut it up for you, dear? *(Over her shoulder)* Gertrude, I forgot the jelly. You know—on the top shelf. Mother Bayard, I found your mother's gravy boat while we were moving. What was her name, dear? What were all your names? You were . . . a . . . Genevieve Wainright. Now your mother—

MOTHER BAYARD. Yes, you must write it down somewhere. I was Genevieve Wainright. My mother was Faith Morrison. She was the daughter of a farmer in New Hampshire who was something of a blacksmith too. And she married young John Wainright—

LUCIA. *(Memorizing on her fingers)* Genevieve Wainright. Faith Morrison.

RODERICK. It's all down in a book somewhere upstairs. We have it all. All that kind of thing is very interesting. Come, Lucia, just a little wine. Mother, a little red wine for Christmas day. Full of iron. "Take a little wine for thy stomach's sake."

LUCIA. Really, I can't get used to wine! What would my father say? But I suppose it's all right.

(Enter COUSIN BRANDON *from the hall. He takes his place by* LUCIA*)*

COUSIN BRANDON. *(Rubbing his hands)* Well, well, I smell turkey. My dear cousins, I can't tell you how pleasant it is to be having Christmas dinner with you all. I've lived out there in Alaska so long without relatives. Let me see, how long have you had this new house, Roderick?

RODERICK. Why, it must be . . .

MOTHER BAYARD. Five years. It's five years, children. You should keep a diary. This is your sixth Christmas dinner here.

LUCIA. Think of that, Roderick. We feel as though we had lived here twenty years.

COUSIN BRANDON. At all events it still looks as good as new.

RODERICK. *(Over his carving)* What'll you have, Brandon, light or dark?—Frieda, fill up Cousin Brandon's glass.

LUCIA. Oh, dear, I can't get used to these wines. I don't know what my father'd say, I'm sure. What'll you have, Mother Bayard?

(During the following speeches MOTHER BAYARD'S *chair, without any visible propulsion, starts to draw away from the table, turns toward the right, and slowly goes toward the Right portal)*

MOTHER BAYARD. Yes, I can remember when there were Indians on this very land.

LUCIA. *(Softly)* Mother Bayard hasn't been very well lately, Roderick.

MOTHER BAYARD. My mother was a Faith Morrison. And in New Hampshire she married a young John Wainright, who was a Congregational minister. He saw her in his congregation one day . . .

LUCIA. *(Rising and coming to Center stage)* Mother Bayard, hadn't you better lie down, dear?

MOTHER BAYARD. . . . and right in the middle of his sermon he said to himself: "I'll marry that girl." And he did, and I'm their daughter. *(*RODERICK *rises, turns to Right with concern)*

LUCIA. *(Looking after her with anxiety)* Just a little nap, dear?

MOTHER BAYARD. I'm all right. Just go on with your dinner. *(Exit right)* I was ten, and I said to my brother . . .

(A very slight pause during which RODERICK *sits and* LUCIA *returns to her seat. All three resume eating.)*

COUSIN BRANDON. *(Genially)* It's too bad it's such a cold dark day today. We almost need the lamps. I spoke to Major Lewis for a moment after church. His sciatica troubles him, but he does pretty well.

LUCIA. *(Dabbing her eyes)* I know Mother Bayard wouldn't want us to grieve for her on Christmas Day, but I can't forget her sitting in her wheelchair right beside us, only a year ago. And she would be so glad to know our good news.

RODERICK. Now, now. It's Christmas. *(Formally)* Cousin Brandon, a glass of wine with you, sir.

COUSIN BRANDON. *(Half rising, lifting his glass gallantly)* A glass of wine with you, sir.

LUCIA. Does the Major's sciatica cause him much pain?

COUSIN BRANDON. Some, perhaps. But you know his way. He says it'll be all the same in a hundred years.

LUCIA. Yes, he's a great philosopher.

RODERICK. His wife sends you a thousand thanks for her Christmas present.

LUCIA. I forget what I gave her.—Oh, yes, the workbasket!

(Slight pause. Characters look toward the Left portal. Through the entrance of Birth comes a nurse holding in her arms an imaginary baby. LUCIA *rushes toward it, the men following)*

LUCIA. O my wonderful new baby, my darling baby! Who ever saw such a child! Quick, nurse, a boy or a girl? A boy! Roderick, what shall we call him? Really, nurse, you've never seen such a child!

RODERICK. We'll call him Charles after your father and grandfather.

LUCIA. But there are no Charleses in the Bible, Roderick.

RODERICK. Of course, there are. Surely there are.

LUCIA. Roderick!—Very well, but he will always be Samuel to me.

COUSIN BRANDON. Really, Nurse, you've never seen such a child.

(NURSE *starts up stage to Center door.)*

LUCIA. What miraculous hands he has! Really, they are the most beautiful hands in the world. All right, nurse. Have a good nap, my darling child.

(Exit NURSE *in the hall.* LUCIA *and* COUSIN BRANDON *to seats.)*

RODERICK. *(Calling through Center door)* Don't drop him, nurse. Brandon and I need him in our firm. Lucia, a little white meat? Some stuffing? Cranberry sauce, anybody?

LUCIA. *(Over her shoulder)* Margaret, the stuffing is very good today.—Just a little, thank you.

RODERICK. Now something to wash it down. *(Half rising)* Cousin Brandon, a glass of wine with you, sir. To the ladies, God bless them.

LUCIA. Thank you, kind sirs.

COUSIN BRANDON. Pity it's such an overcast day today. And no snow.

LUCIA. But the sermon was lovely. I cried and cried. Dr. Spaulding does preach such a splendid sermon.

RODERICK. I saw Major Lewis for a moment after church. He says his rheumatism comes and goes. His wife says she has something for Charles and will bring it over this afternoon.

(Again they turn to the portal down Left. Enter NURSE *as before.* LUCIA *rushes to her.* RODERICK *comes to Center of stage below table.* COUSIN BRANDON *does not rise.)*

LUCIA. O my lovely new baby! Really, it never occurred to me that it might be a girl. Why, nurse, she's perfect.

RODERICK. Now call her what you choose. It's your turn.

LUCIA. Loolooolooloo. Aië. Aië. Yes, this time I shall have my way. She shall be called Genevieve after your mother. Have a good nap, my treasure.

(Exit NURSE *into the hall.)*

Imagine! Sometime she'll be grown up and say "Good morning, Mother. Good morning, Father."—Really, Cousin Brandon, you don't find a baby like that every day.

(They return to their seats and again begin to eat. RODERICK *carves as before, standing.)*

COUSIN BRANDON. *And* the new factory.

LUCIA. A new factory? Really? Roderick, I shall be very uncomfortable if we're going to turn out to be rich. I've been afraid of that for years.—However, we mustn't talk about such things on Christmas Day. I'll just take a little piece of white meat, thank you. Roderick, Charles is destined for the ministry. I'm sure of it.

RODERICK. Woman, he's only twelve. Let him have a free mind. *We* want him in the firm, I don't mind saying. *(He sits. Definitely shows maturity.)* Anyway, no time passes as slowly as this when you're waiting for your urchins to grow up and settle down to business.

LUCIA. I don't want time to go any faster, thank you. I love the children just as they are.—Really, Roderick, you know what the doctor said: one glass a meal. No, Margaret, that will be all.

*(*RODERICK *rises, glass in hand. With a look of dismay on his face he takes a few steps toward the Right portal)*

RODERICK. *(Glass in hand)* Now I wonder what's the matter with me.

LUCIA. Roderick, do be reasonable.

RODERICK. *(Rises, takes a few steps Right with gallant irony)* But, my dear, statistics show that we steady, moderate drinkers . . .

LUCIA. *(Rises, rushes to Center below table)* Roderick! My dear! What . . . ?

RODERICK. *(Returns to his seat with a frightened look of relief; now definitely older)* Well, it's fine to be back at table with you again.

*(*LUCIA *returns to her seat)*

How many good Christmas dinners have I had to miss upstairs? And to be back at a fine bright one, too.

LUCIA. O my dear, you gave us a very alarming time! Here's your glass of milk.—Josephine, bring Mr. Bayard his medicine from the cupboard in the library.

RODERICK. At all events, now that I'm better I'm going to start doing something about the house.

LUCIA. Roderick! You're not going to change the house?

RODERICK Only touch it up here and there. It looks a hundred years old.

*(*CHARLES *enters casually from the hall)*

CHARLES. It's a great blowy morning, Mother. The wind comes over the hill like a lot of cannon. *(He kisses his mother's hair)*

LUCIA Charles, you carve the turkey, dear. Your father's not well.

CHARLES. You always said you hated carving, though you are so clever at it.

*(*CHARLES *gets a chair from Right wall and puts it Right end of table where* MOTHER BAYARD *was.* RODERICK *sits.* CHARLES *takes his father's former place at the end of the table.* CHARLES, *sitting, begins to carve.)*

LUCIA. *(Showing her years)* And such a good sermon. I cried and cried. Mother Bayard loved a good sermon so. And she used to sing the Christmas hymns all around the year. Oh, dear, oh, dear, I've been thinking of her all morning!

CHARLES. Shh, Mother. It's Christmas Day. You mustn't think of such things. You mustn't be depressed.

LUCIA. But sad things aren't the same as depressing things. I must be getting old: I like them.

CHARLES. Uncle Brandon, you haven't anything to eat. Pass his plate, Hilda . . . and some cranberry sauce . . .

(Enter GENEVIEVE *from the hall.)*

GENEVIEVE. It's glorious. *(Kisses father's temple, gets chair and sits Center between her father and* COUSIN BRANDON.*)* Every last twig is wrapped around with ice. You almost never see that.

LUCIA. Did you have time to deliver those presents after church, Genevieve?

GENEVIEVE. Yes, Mama. Old Mrs. Lewis sends you a thousand thanks for hers. It was just what she wanted, she said. Give me lots, Charles, lots.

RODERICK. Statistics, ladies and gentlemen, show that we steady, moderate . . .

CHARLES. How about a little skating this afternoon, Father?

RODERICK. I'll live till I'm ninety. *(Rising and starting toward Right portal)*

LUCIA. I really don't think he ought to go skating.

RODERICK. *(At the very portal, suddenly astonished)* Yes, but . . . but . . . not yet!

(He goes out)

LUCIA. *(Dabbing her eyes)* He was so young and so clever, Cousin Brandon. *(Raising her voice for* COUSIN BRANDON*'s deafness)* I say he was so young and so clever.—Never forget your father, children. He was a good man. Well, he wouldn't want us to grieve for him today.

CHARLES. White or dark, Genevieve? Just another sliver, Mother?

LUCIA. *(Drawing on her shawl)* I can remember our first Christmas dinner in this house, Genevieve. Twenty-five years ago today. Mother Bayard was sitting here in her wheelchair. She could remember when Indians lived on this very spot and when she had to cross the river on a new-made raft.

CHARLES. She couldn't have, Mother.

GENEVIEVE. That can't be true.

LUCIA. It certainly was true—even I can remember when there was only one paved street. We were very happy to walk on boards. *(Louder, to* COUSIN BRANDON*)* We can remember when there were no sidewalks, can't we, Cousin Brandon?

COUSIN BRANDON. *(Delighted)* Oh, yes! And those were the days.

CHARLES & GENEVIEVE. *(Sotto voce, this is a family refrain)* Those were the days.

LUCIA. . . . and the ball last night, Genevieve? Did you have a nice time? I hope you didn't *waltz,* dear. I think a girl in our position ought to set an example. Did Charles keep an eye on you?

GENEVIEVE. HE had none left. They were all on Leonora Banning. He can't conceal it any longer, Mother. I think he's engaged to marry Leonora Banning.

CHARLES. I'm not engaged to marry anyone.

LUCIA. Well, she's very pretty.

GENEVIEVE. I shall never marry, Mother.—I shall sit in this house beside you forever, as though life were one long, happy Christmas dinner.

LUCIA. O my child, you mustn't say such things!

GENEVIEVE. *(Playfully)* You don't want me? You don't want me?

*(*LUCIA *bursts into tears.* GENEVIEVE *rises and goes to her.)*

Why, Mother, how silly you are! There's nothing sad about that—what could possibly be sad about that?

LUCIA. *(Drying her eyes)* Forgive me. I'm just unpredictable, that's all.

*(*CHARLES *goes to the door and leads in* LEONORA BANNING *from the hall.)*

CHARLES. Leonora!

LEONORA. Good morning, Mother Bayard.

*(*LUCIA *rises and greets* LEONORA *near the door.* COUSIN BRANDON *also rises.)*

Good morning, everybody. Mother Bayard, you sit here by Charles. *(She helps her into chair formerly occupied by* RODERICK. COUSIN BRANDON *sits in Center chair.* GENEVIEVE *sits on his Left, and* LEONORA *sits at foot of the table.)* It's really a splendid Christmas Day today.

CHARLES. Little white meat? Genevieve, Mother, Leonora?

LEONORA. Every last twig is encircled with ice.—You never see that.

CHARLES. *(Shouting)* Uncle Brandon, another?—Rogers, fill my uncle's glass.

LUCIA. *(To* CHARLES*)* Do what your father used to do. It would please Cousin Brandon so. You know *(Pretending to raise a glass)* "Uncle Brandon, a glass of wine . . ."

CHARLES. *(Rising)* Uncle Brandon, a glass of wine with you, sir.

COUSIN BRANDON. A glass of wine with you, sir. To the ladies, God bless them every one.

THE LADIES. Thank you, kind sirs.

GENEVIEVE. And if I go to Germany for my music I promise to be back for Christmas. I wouldn't miss that.

LUCIA. I hate to think of you over there all alone in those strange pensions.

GENEVIEVE. But, darling, the time will pass so fast that you'll hardly know I'm gone. I'll be back in the twinkling of an eye.

*(*LEONORA *looks toward Left portal, rises, takes several steps.* NURSE *enters, with baby, down Left.)*

LEONORA. Oh, what an angel! The darlingest baby in the world. Do let me hold it, nurse.

(The NURSE *resolutely has been crossing the stage and now exits at the Right portal.* LEONORA *follows.)*

Oh, I did love it so!

*(*CHARLES *rises, puts his arm around his wife, whispering, and slowly leads her back to her chair.)*

GENEVIEVE. *(Softly to her mother as the other two cross)* Isn't there anything I can do?

LUCIA. *(Raises her eyebrows, ruefully)* No, dear. Only time, only the passing of time can help in these things.

*(*CHARLES *returns to his seat. Slight pause.)*

Don't you think we could ask Cousin Ermengarde to come and live with us here? There's plenty for everyone and there's no reason why she should go on teaching the first grade for ever and ever. She wouldn't be in the way, would she, Charles?

CHARLES. No, I think it would be fine.—A little more potato and gravy, anybody? A little more turkey, Mother?

*(*COUSIN BRANDON *rises and starts slowly toward the Right portal.* LUCIA *rises and stands for a moment with her face in her hands)*

COUSIN BRANDON. *(Muttering)* It was great to be in Alaska in those days . . .

GENEVIEVE. *(Half rising, and gazing at her mother in fear)* Mother, what is . . . ?

LUCIA. *(Hurriedly)* Hush, my dear. It will pass.—Hold fast to your music, you know. *(As* GENEVIEVE *starts toward her)* No, no. I want to be alone for a few minutes.

CHARLES. If the Republicans collected all their votes instead of going off into cliques among themselves, they might prevent his getting a second term.

*(*LUCIA *turns and starts after* COUSIN BRANDON *toward the right.)*

GENEVIEVE. Charles, Mother doesn't tell us, but she hasn't been very well these days.

CHARLES. Come, Mother, we'll go to Florida for a few weeks.

*(*GENEVIEVE *rushes toward her mother.)*

(Exit COUSIN BRANDON *Right.)*

LUCIA. *(By the portal, smiling at* GENEVIEVE *and waving her hand)* Don't be foolish. Don't grieve.

*(*LUCIA *clasps her hands under her chin. Her lips move, whispering. She walks serenely into the portal.)*

GENEVIEVE. *(Stares after her)* But what will I do? What's left for me to do? *(She returns to her seat.)*

(At the same moment the NURSE, *with two babies, enters from the left.* LEONORA *rushes to it)*

LEONORA. O my darlings . . . twins . . . Charles, aren't they glorious! Look at them. Look at them. *(*CHARLES *crosses down Left.)*

CHARLES. *(Bending over the basket)* Which is which?

LEONORA. I feel as though I were the first mother who ever had twins.—Look at them now! But why wasn't Mother Bayard allowed to stay and see them!

GENEVIEVE. *(Rising suddenly distraught, loudly)* I don't want to go on. I can't bear it.

CHARLES. *(Goes to her quickly. They sit down. He whispers to her earnestly, taking both her hands)* But Genevieve, Genevieve! How frightfully Mother would feel to think that . . . Genevieve!

GENEVIEVE. *(Wildly)* I never told her how wonderful she was. We all treated her as though she were just a friend in the house. I thought she'd be here forever. *(Sits)*

LEONORA. *(Timidly)* Genevieve darling, do come one minute and hold my babies' hands.

*(*GENEVIEVE *collects herself and goes over to the* NURSE. *She smiles brokenly into the basket)*

We shall call the girl Lucia after her grandmother—will that please you? Do just see what adorable little hands they have.

GENEVIEVE. They are wonderful, Leonora.

LEONORA. Give him your finger, darling. Just let him hold it.

CHARLES. And we'll call the boy Samuel.—Well, now everybody come and finish your dinners. *(The women take their places.* CHARLES *calls out into the hall.)* Don't drop them, nurse; at least don't drop the boy. We need him in the firm. *(He returns to his place.)*

LEONORA. Someday they'll be big. Imagine! They'll come in and say "Hello, Mother!"

CHARLES. *(Now forty, dignified)* Come, a little wine, Leonora, Genevieve? Full of iron. Eduardo, fill the ladies' glasses. It certainly is a keen, cold morning. I used to go skating with Father on mornings like this and Mother would come back from church saying—

GENEVIEVE. *(Dreamily)* I know: saying, "Such a splendid sermon. I cried and cried."

LEONORA. Why did she cry, dear?

GENEVIEVE. That generation all cried at sermons. It was their way.

LEONORA. Really, Genevieve?

GENEVIEVE. They had had to go since they were children and I suppose sermons reminded them of their fathers and mothers, just as Christmas dinners do us. Especially in an old house like this.

LEONORA. It really is pretty old, Charles. And so ugly, with all that ironwork filigree and that dreadful cupola.

GENEVIEVE. Charles! You aren't going to change the house!

CHARLES. No, no. I won't give up the house, but great heavens! It's fifty years old. This spring we'll remove the cupola and build a new wing toward the tennis courts.

(From now on GENEVIEVE *is seen to change. She sits up more straightly. The corners of her mouth become fixed. She becomes a forthright and slightly disillusioned spinster.* CHARLES *becomes the plain businessman and a little pompous)*

LEONORA. And then couldn't we ask your dear old Cousin Ermengarde to come and live with us? She's really the self-effacing kind.

CHARLES Ask her now. Take her out of the first grade.

GENEVIEVE. We only seem to think of it on Christmas Day with her Christmas card staring us in the face.

(Enter Left, NURSE *and baby.)*

LEONORA. Another boy! Another boy! Here's a Roderick for you at last.

CHARLES. *(Crossing down Left)* Roderick Brandon Bayard. A regular little fighter.

LEONORA. Goodbye, darling. Don't grow up too fast. Yes, yes. Aie, aie, aie—stay just as you are. Thank you, nurse.

GENEVIEVE. *(Who has not left the table, repeats dryly)* Stay just as you are.

(Exit NURSE *into the hall.* CHARLES *and* LEONORA *return to their places)*

LEONORA. Now I have three children. One, two, three. Two boys and a girl. I'm collecting them. It's very exciting. *(Over her shoulder)* What, Hilda? Oh, Cousin Ermengarde's come! Come in, Cousin.

(She goes to the hall door and welcomes COUSIN ERMENGARDE, *already an elderly woman.)*

ERMENGARDE. *(Shyly)* It's such a pleasure to be with you all.

CHARLES. *(Pulling out the Center chair for her)* The twins have taken a great fancy to you already, Cousin.

LEONORA. The baby went to her at once.

CHARLES. Exactly how are we related, Cousin Ermengarde?—There, Genevieve, that's your specialty.—First a little more turkey and stuffing, Mother? Cranberry sauce, anybody?

GENEVIEVE. I can work it out: Grandmother Bayard was your . . .

ERMENGARDE. Your Grandmother Bayard was a second cousin of my Grandmother Haskins through the Wainrights.

CHARLES. Well, it's all in a book somewhere upstairs. All that kind of thing is awfully interesting.

GENEVIEVE. Nonsense. There are no such books. I collect my notes off gravestones, and you have to scrape a good deal of moss—let me tell you—to find one great-grandparent.

CHARLES There's a story that my Grandmother Bayard crossed the Mississippi on a raft before there were any bridges or ferryboats. She died before Genevieve and I were born. Time certainly goes very fast in a great new country like this. Have some more cranberry sauce, Cousin Ermengarde.

ERMENGARDE. *(Timidly)* Well, time must be passing very slowly in Europe with this dreadful, dreadful war going on.

CHARLES. Perhaps an occasional war isn't so bad after all. It clears up a lot of poisons that collect in nations. It's like a boil.

ERMENGARDE. Oh, dear, oh, dear!

CHARLES. *(With relish)* Yes, it's like a boil.—Ho! Ho! Here are your twins.

(The twins appear at the door into the hall. SAM *is wearing the uniform of an ensign.* LUCIA *is fussing over some detail on it)*

LUCIA. Isn't he wonderful in it, Mother?

CHARLES. Let's get a look at you.

SAM. Mother, don't let Roderick fool with my stamp album while I'm gone. *(Crosses to the Right)*

LEONORA. Now, Sam, do write a letter once in a while. Do be a good boy about that, mind.

SAM. You might send some of those cakes of yours once in a while, Cousin Ermengarde.

*(*LEONORA *rises)*

ERMENGARDE. *(In a flutter)* I certainly will, my dear boy.

*(*LEONORA *crosses to Center.* SAM *crosses down Right.)*

CHARLES. *(Rising and facing* SAM.*)* If you need any money, we have agents in Paris and London, remember.

LEONORA. *(Crossing down Right)* Do be a good boy, Sam.

SAM. Well, good-bye . . .

*(*SAM *kisses his mother without sentimentality and goes out*

briskly through the Right portal. They all return to their seats, LUCIA *sitting at her father's left.)*

ERMENGARDE. *(In a low, constrained voice, making conversation)* I spoke to Mrs. Fairchild for a moment coming out of church. Her rheumatism's a little better, she says. She sends you her warmest thanks for the Christmas present. The workbasket, wasn't it? *(Slight pause)*—It was an admirable sermon. And our stained-glass window looked so beautiful, Leonora, so beautiful. Everybody spoke of it and so affectionately of Sammy. *(*LEONORA*'s hand goes to her mouth)* Forgive me, Leonora, but it's better to speak of him than not to speak of him when we're all thinking of him so hard.

LEONORA. *(Rising, in anguish)* He was a mere boy. He was a mere boy, Charles.

CHARLES. My dear, my dear.

LEONORA. I want to tell him how wonderful he was. We let him go so casually. I want to tell him how we all feel about him.—Forgive me, let me walk about a minute.—Yes, of course, Ermengarde—it's best to speak of him.

LUCIA. *(In a low voice to* GENEVIEVE*)* Isn't there anything I can do?

GENEVIEVE. No, no. Only time, only the passing of time can help in these things.

*(*LEONORA*, straying about the room, finds herself near the door to the hall at the moment that her son* RODERICK *enters. He links his arm with hers and leads her back to the table. He looks up and sees the family's dejection.)*

RODERICK. What's the matter, anyway? What are you so glum about? The skating was fine today.

CHARLES. Roderick, I have something to say to you.

RODERICK. *(Standing below his mother's chair)* Everybody was there. Lucia skated in the corners with Dan Creighton the whole time. When'll it be, Lucia, when'll it be?

LUCIA. I don't know what you mean.

RODERICK. Lucia's leaving us soon, Mother. Dan Creighton, of all people.

CHARLES. *(Ominously)* Young man, I have something to say to you.

RODERICK. Yes, Father.

CHARLES. Is it true, Roderick, that you made yourself conspicuous last night at the Country Club—at a Christmas Eve dance, too?

LEONORA. Not now, Charles, I beg of you. This is Christmas dinner.

RODERICK. *(Loudly)* No, I didn't.

LUCIA. Really, Father, he didn't. It was that dreadful Johnny Lewis.

CHARLES. I don't want to hear about Johnny Lewis. I want to know whether a son of mine . . .

LEONORA. Charles, I beg of you . . .

CHARLES. The first family of this city!

RODERICK. *(Crossing below table to Left Center)* I hate this town and everything about it. I always did.

CHARLES. You behaved like a spoiled puppy, sir, an ill-bred spoiled puppy.

RODERICK. What did I do? What did I do that was wrong?

CHARLES. *(Rising)* You were drunk and you were rude to the daughters of my best friends.

GENEVIEVE. *(Striking the table)* Nothing in the world deserves an ugly scene like this. Charles, I'm ashamed of you.

RODERICK. Great God, you gotta get drunk in this town to forget how dull it is. Time passes so slowly here that it stands still, that's what's the trouble. *(Turns and walks toward the hall door)*

CHARLES. Well, young man, we can employ your time. You will leave the university and you will come into the Bayard factory on January second.

RODERICK. *(At the door into the hall)* I have better things to do than to go into your old factory. I'm going somewhere where time passes, my God!

(He goes out into the hall)

LEONORA. *(Rising and rushing to the door)* Roderick, Roderick, come here just a moment.—Charles where can he go?

LUCIA. *(Rising)* Shh, Mother. He'll come back. *(She leads her mother back to chair then starts for the hall door)* Now I have to go upstairs and pack my trunk.

LEONORA. I won't have any children left! *(Sits)*

LUCIA. *(From the door)* Shh, Mother. He'll come back. He's only gone to California or somewhere. Cousin Ermengarde has done most of my packing—thanks a thousand times, Cousin Ermengarde. *(She kisses her mother as an afterthought)* I won't be long.

(She runs out into the hall)

ERMENGARDE. *(Cheerfully)* It's a very beautiful day. On the way home from church I stopped and saw Mrs. Foster a moment. Her arthritis comes and goes.

LEONORA. Is she actually in pain, dear?

ERMENGARDE. Oh, she says it'll all be the same in a hundred years!

LEONORA. Yes, she's a brave little stoic.

CHARLES. Come now, a little white meat, Mother?—Mary, pass my cousin's plate.

LEONORA. What is it, Mary?—Oh, here's a telegram from them in Paris! "Love and Christmas greetings to all." I told them we'd be eating some of their wedding cake and thinking about them today. It seems to be all decided that they will settle down in the east, Ermengarde. I can't even have my daughter for a neighbor. They hope to build before long somewhere on the shore north of New York.

GENEVIEVE. There is no shore north of New York.

LEONORA. Well, east or west or whatever it is.

(Pause)

CHARLES. *(Now sixty years old)* My, what a dark day. How slowly time passes without any young people in the house.

LEONORA. I have three children somewhere.

CHARLES. *(Blunderingly offering comfort)* Well, one of them gave his life for his country.

LEONORA. *(Sadly)* And one of them is selling aluminum in China.

GENEVIEVE. *(Slowly working herself up to a hysterical crisis)* I can stand everything but this terrible soot everywhere. We should have moved long ago. We're surrounded by factories. We have to change the window curtains every week.

LEONORA. Why, Genevieve!

GENEVIEVE. I can't stand it. *(Rising)* I can't stand it any more. I'm going abroad. It's not only the soot that comes through the very walls of this house; it's the *thoughts*, it's the thought of what has been and what might have been here. And the feeling about this house of the years *grinding away*. My mother died yesterday—not twenty-five years ago. Oh, I'm going to live and die abroad! *(CHARLES rises.)* Yes, I'm going to be the American old maid living and dying in a pension in Munich or Florence.

ERMENGARDE. Genevieve, you're tired.

CHARLES. Come, Genevieve, take a good drink of cold water. Mary, open the window a minute.

GENEVIEVE. I'm sorry. I'm sorry.

(GENEVIEVE hurries tearfully out into the hall. CHARLES sits.)

ERMENGARDE. Dear Genevieve will come back to us, I think.

(She rises and starts toward the Right portal)

You should have been out today, Leonora. It was one of those days when everything was encircled with ice. Very pretty, indeed.

CHARLES. Leonora, I used to go skating with Father on mornings like this. I wish I felt a little better.

(CHARLES *rises and starts following* ERMENGARDE *toward the Right.)*

LEONORA. *(Rising)* What! Have I got two invalids on my hands at once? Now, Cousin Ermengarde, you must get better and help me nurse Charles.

ERMENGARDE. I'll do my best.

(ERMENGARDE *turns at the very portal and comes back to the table)*

CHARLES. Well, Leonora, I'll do what you ask. I'll write the puppy a letter of forgiveness and apology. It's Christmas Day. I'll cable it. That's what I'll do.

(He goes out the portal Right. Slight pause.)

LEONORA. *(Drying her eyes)* Ermengarde, it's such a comfort having you here with me. *(Sits in place at left of* ERMENGARDE, *formerly occupied by* GENEVIEVE.*)* Mary, I really can't eat anything. Well, perhaps, a sliver of white meat.

ERMENGARDE. *(Very old)* I spoke to Mrs. Keene for a moment coming out of church. She asked after the young people.—At church I felt very proud sitting under our windows, Leonora, and our brass tablets. The Bayard aisle—it's a regular Bayard aisle and I love it.

LEONORA. Ermengarde, would you be very angry with me if I went and stayed with the young people a little this spring?

ERMENGARDE. Why, no. I know how badly they want you and need you. Especially now that they're about to build a new house.

LEONORA. You wouldn't be angry? This house is yours as long as you want it, remember.

ERMENGARDE. I don't see why the rest of you dislike it. I like it more than I can say.

LEONORA. I won't be long. I'll be back in no time and we can have some more of our readings aloud in the evening.

(She kisses her and goes into the hall)

(ERMENGARDE, *left alone, eats slowly and talks to Mary)*

ERMENGARDE. Really, Mary, I'll change my mind. If you'll ask Bertha to be good enough to make me a little eggnog. A dear little eggnog.—Such a nice letter this morning from Mrs. Bayard, Mary. Such a nice letter. They're having their first Christmas dinner in the new house. They must be very happy. They call her Mother Bayard, she says, as though she were an old lady. And she says she finds it more comfortable to come and go in a wheelchair.—Such a dear letter . . . And Mary, I can tell you a secret. It's still a great secret, mind! They're expecting a grandchild. Isn't that good news! Now I'll read a little.

(She props a book up before her, still dipping a spoon into a custard from time to time. She grows from very old to immensely old. She sighs. She finds a cane beside her, and totters out of the Right portal, murmuring.)

(The audience gazes for a space of time at the table before the lights slowly dim out.)

"Dear little Roderick and little Lucia."

End of Play

The Happy Journey to Trenton and Camden

Notes to the Producer

Although the speech, manner and business of the actors is colloquial and realistic, the production should stimulate the imagination and be implied and suggestive. All properties, except two, are imaginary, but their use is to be carried with detailed pantomime. One of these two is the automobile, which is made up of four chairs on a low platform. In some productions, because of the sight lines of the auditorium, it has been found necessary to raise slightly the two rear chairs of the automobile. The second is an ordinary cot or couch.

The Stage Manager not only moves forward and withdraws these two properties, but he reads from a typescript the lines of all the minor (invisible) characters. He reads them clearly, but with little attempt at characterization, even when he responds in the person of a child or a woman. He may smoke, read a newspaper and eat an apple throughout the course of the play. He should never be obtrusive nor distract the attention of the audience from the central action.

It should constantly be borne in mind that the purpose of this play is the portrayal of the character of Ma Kirby, the author at one time having even considered entitling the play "The Portrait of a Lady." Accordingly, the director should constantly keep in mind that Ma Kirby's humor, strength and humanity constitute the unifying element throughout. This aspect should always rise above the merely humorous characteristic details of the play.

Many productions have fallen into two regrettable extremes. On the one hand actors have exaggerated the humorous characters and situations in the direction of farce; and on the other hand, have treated Ma Kirby's sentiment and religion with sentimentality and preachy solemnity. The atmosphere, comedy, and characterization of this play are most effective when they are handled with great simplicity and evenness.

Thornton Wilder, 1931

Characters

THE STAGE MANAGER

MA, MRS. KATE KIRBY

ARTHUR, THIRTEEN, HER SON

CAROLINE, FIFTEEN, HER DAUGHTER

PA

BEULAH, TWENTY-TWO, THE KIRBYS' MARRIED DAUGHTER WHO LIVES IN CAMDEN, NEW JERSEY

Setting

The Kirby house; then the Kirby family car trip from Newark to Camden, New Jersey.

(No scenery is required for this play. The idea is that no place is being represented. This may be achieved by a gray curtain back-drop with no side-pieces; a cyclorama; or the empty bare stage.)

(As the curtain rises, THE STAGE MANAGER *is leaning lazily against the proscenium pillar at the audience's left. He is smoking.)*

*(*ARTHUR *is playing marbles in the center of the stage in pantomime.)*

*(*CAROLINE *is at the remote back right talking to some girls who are invisible to us.)*

*(*MA KIRBY *is anxiously putting on her hat [real] before an imaginary mirror.)*

MA. Where's your pa? Why isn't he here? I declare we'll never get started.

ARTHUR. Ma, where's my hat? I guess I don't go if I can't find my hat. *(Still playing marbles)*

MA. Go out into the hall and see if it isn't there. Where's Caroline gone to now, the plagued child?

ARTHUR. She's out waitin' in the street talkin' to the Jones girls.—I just looked in the hall a thousand times, Ma, and it isn't there. *(He spits for good luck before a difficult shot and mutters)* Come on, baby.

MA. Go and look again, I say. Look carefully.

*(*ARTHUR *rises, runs to the right, turns around swiftly, re-*

turns to his game, flinging himself on the floor with a terrible impact and starts shooting an aggie.)

ARTHUR. No, Ma, it's not there.

MA. *(Serenely)* Well, you don't leave Newark without that hat, make up your mind to that. I don't go no journeys with a hoodlum.

ARTHUR. Aw, Ma!

(MA *comes down to the footlights and talks toward the audience as through a window.)*

MA. *(Calling)* Oh, Mrs. Schwartz!

THE STAGE MANAGER. *(Consulting his script)* Here I am, Mrs. Kirby. Are you going yet?

MA. I guess we're going in just a minute. How's the baby?

THE STAGE MANAGER. She's all right now. We slapped her on the back and she spat it up.

MA. Isn't that fine!—Well now, if you'll be good enough to give the cat a saucer of milk in the morning and the evening, Mrs. Schwartz, I'll be ever so grateful to you.—Oh, good afternoon, Mrs. Hobmeyer!

THE STAGE MANAGER. Good afternoon, Mrs. Kirby, I hear you're going away.

MA. *(Modest)* Oh, just for three days, Mrs. Hobmeyer, to see my married daughter, Beulah, in Camden. Elmer's got his vacation week from the laundry early this year, and he's just the best driver in the world.

(CAROLINE *comes "into the house" and stands by her mother)*

THE STAGE MANAGER. Is the whole family going?

MA. Yes, all four of us that's here. The change ought to be good for the children. My married daughter was downright sick a while ago—

THE STAGE MANAGER. Tchk-Tchk-Tchk! Yes. I remember you tellin' us.

MA. And I just want to go down and see the child. I ain't seen her since then. I just won't rest easy in my mind without I see her. *(To* CAROLINE*)* Can't you say good afternoon to Mrs. Hobmeyer?

CAROLINE. *(Blushes and lowers her eyes and says woodenly)* Good afternoon, Mrs. Hobmeyer.

THE STAGE MANAGER. Good afternoon, dear.—Well, I'll wait and beat these rugs after you're gone, because I don't want to choke you. I hope you have a good time and find everything all right.

MA. Thank you, Mrs. Hobmeyer, I hope I will.—Well, I guess that milk for the cat is all, Mrs. Schwartz, if you're sure you don't mind. If anything should come up, the key to the back door is hanging by the icebox.

CAROLINE. Ma! Not so loud.

ARTHUR. Everybody can hear yuh.

MA. Stop pullin' my dress, children. *(In a loud whisper)* The key to the back door I'll leave hangin' by the icebox and I'll leave the screen door unhooked.

THE STAGE MANAGER. Now have a good trip, dear, and give my love to Loolie.

MA. I will, and thank you a thousand times.

(She lowers the window, turns up stage and looks around. CAROLINE *goes Left and vigorously rubs her cheeks.* MA *occupies herself with the last touches of packing.)*

What can be keeping your pa?

ARTHUR. *(Who has not left his marbles)* I can't find my hat, Ma.

(Enter ELMER *holding a hat.)*

ELMER. Here's Arthur's hat. He musta left it in the car Sunday.

MA. That's a mercy. Now we can start.—Caroline Kirby, what you done to your cheeks?

CAROLINE. *(Defiant, abashed)* Nothin'.

MA. If you've put anything on 'em, I'll slap you.

CAROLINE. No, Ma, of course I haven't. *(Hanging her head)* I just rubbed 'em to make 'em red. All the girls do that at high school when they're goin' places.

MA. Such silliness I never saw. Elmer, what kep' you?

ELMER. *(Always even-voiced and always looking out a little anxiously through his spectacles)* I just went to the garage and had Charlie give a last look at it, Kate.

MA. I'm glad you did. *(Collecting two pieces of imaginary luggage and starting for the door.)* I wouldn't like to have no breakdown miles from anywhere. Now we can start. Arthur, put those marbles away. Anybody'd think you didn't want to go on a journey to look at yuh.

(They go out through the "hall," take the short steps that denote going downstairs, and find themselves in the street.)

ELMER. Here, you boys, you keep away from that car.

MA. Those Sullivan boys put their heads into everything.

*(*THE STAGE MANAGER *has moved forward four chairs and a low platform. This is the automobile. It is in the center of the stage and faces the audience. The platform slightly raises the two chairs in the rear.* PA'*s hands hold an imaginary steering wheel and continually shift gears.* CAROLINE *sits beside him.* ARTHUR *is behind him and* MA *behind* CAROLINE.*)*

CAROLINE. *(Self-consciously)* Good-bye, Mildred. Good-bye, Helen.

THE STAGE MANAGER. Good-bye, Caroline. Good-bye, Mrs. Kirby. I hope y'have a good time.

MA. Good-bye, girls.

THE STAGE MANAGER. Good-bye, Kate. The car looks fine.

MA. *(Looking upward toward a window)* Oh, good-bye, Emma! *(Modestly)* We think it's the best little Chevrolet in the world.—Oh, good-bye, Mrs. Adler!

THE STAGE MANAGER. What, are you going away, Mrs. Kirby?

MA. Just for three days, Mrs. Adler, to see my married daughter in Camden.

THE STAGE MANAGER. Have a good time.

(Now MA, CAROLINE *and the* STAGE MANAGER *break out into a tremendous chorus of good-byes. The whole street is saying good-bye.* ARTHUR *takes out his peashooter and lets fly happily into the air. There is a lurch or two and they are off)*

ARTHUR. *(In sudden fright)* Pa! Pa! Don't go by the school. Mr. Biedenbach might see us!

MA. I don't care if he does see us. I guess I can take my children out of school for one day without having to hide down back streets about it.

*(*ELMER *nods to a passerby.* MA *asks without sharpness.)*

Who was that you spoke to, Elmer?

ELMER. That was the fellow who arranges our banquets down to the lodge, Kate.

MA. Is he the one who had to buy four hundred steaks? *(*PA *nods)* I declare, I'm glad I'm not him.

ELMER. The air's getting better already. Take deep breaths, children.

(They inhale noisily)

ARTHUR. *(Pointing to a sign and indicating that it gradually goes by)* Gee, it's almost open fields already. *"Weber and*

Heilbronner Suits for Well-Dressed Men." Ma, can I have one of them some day?

MA. If you graduate with good marks perhaps your father'll let you have one for graduation.

(Pause. General gazing about and then a sudden lurch.)

CAROLINE. *(Whining)* Oh, Pa! Do we have to wait while that whole funeral goes by?

(PA takes off his hat. MA cranes forward with absorbed curiosity)

MA. Take off your hat, Arthur. Look at your father.—Why, Elmer, I do believe that's a lodge brother of yours. See the banner? I suppose this is the Elizabeth branch.

(ELMER nods. MA sighs Tchk-tchk-tchk. They all lean forward and watch the funeral in silence, growing momentarily more solemnized. After a pause, MA continues almost dreamily but not sentimentally.)

Well, we haven't forgotten the funeral that we went on, have we? We haven't forgotten our good Harold. He gave his life for his country, we mustn't forget that.

(She passes her finger from the corner of her eye across her cheek. There is another pause, with cheerful resignation.)

MA. Well, we'll all hold up the traffic for a few minutes some day.

THE CHILDREN. *(Very uncomfortable)* Ma!

MA. *(Without self-pity)* Well I'm "ready," children. I hope everybody in this car is "ready."

(She puts her hand on PA's shoulder)

And I pray to go first, Elmer. Yes.

(PA *touches her hand)*

CAROLINE. Ma, everybody's looking at you.

ARTHUR. Everybody's laughing at you.

MA. Oh, hold your tongues! I don't care what a lot of silly people in Elizabeth, New Jersey, think of me.—Now we can go on. That's the last.

(There is another lurch and the car goes on)

CAROLINE. *(Looking at a sign and turning as she passes it) "Fit-Rite Suspenders. The Working Man's Choice."* Pa, why do they spell Rite that way?

ELMER. So, that it'll make you stop and ask about it, Missy.

CAROLINE. Papa, you're teasing me.—Ma, why do they say *"Three Hundred Rooms Three Hundred Baths?"*

ARTHUR. *"Millers Spaghetti: The Family's Favorite Dish."* Ma, why don't you ever have spaghetti?

MA. Go along, you'd never eat it.

ARTHUR. Ma, I like it now.

CAROLINE. *(With gesture)* Yum-yum. It looks wonderful up there. Ma, make some when we get home?

MA. *(Dryly)* "The management is always happy to receive suggestions. We aim to please."

(The whole family finds this exquisitely funny. The children scream with laughter. Even ELMER *smiles.* MA *remains modest)*

ELMER. Well, I guess no one's complaining, Kate. Everybody knows you're a good cook.

MA. I don't know whether I'm a good cook or not, but I know I've had practice. At least I've cooked three meals a day for twenty-five years.

ARTHUR. Aw, Ma, you went out to eat once in a while.

MA. Yes. That made it a leap year.

(This joke is no less successful than its predecessor. When the laughter dies down, CAROLINE *turns around in an ecstasy of well-being, and kneeling on the cushions says.)*

CAROLINE Ma, I love going out in the country like this. Let's do it often, Ma.

MA. Goodness, smell that air will you! It's got the whole ocean in it.—Elmer, drive careful over that bridge. This must be New Brunswick we're coming to.

ARTHUR. *(Jealous of his mother's successes)* Ma, when is the next comfort station?

MA. *(Unruffled)* You don't want one. You just said that to be awful.

CAROLINE. *(Shrilly)* Yes, he did, Ma. He's terrible. He says that kind of thing right out in school and I want to sink through the floor, Ma. He's terrible.

MA. Oh, don't get so excited about nothing, Miss Proper! I guess we're all yewman-beings in this car, at least as far as I know. And, Arthur, you try and be a gentleman.—Elmer, don't run over that collie dog.

(She follows the dog with her eyes)

Looked kinda peaked to me. Needs a good honest bowl of leavings. Pretty dog, too.

(Her eyes fall on a billboard)

That's a pretty advertisement for Chesterfield cigarettes, isn't it? Looks like Beulah, a little.

ARTHUR. Ma?

MA. Yes.

ARTHUR. Can't I take a paper route *("Route" rhymes with "out")* with the *Newark Daily Post?*

MA. No, you cannot. No, sir. I hear they make the paperboys get up at four-thirty in the morning. No son of mine is going to get up at four-thirty every morning, not if it's to make a million dollars. Your *Saturday Evening Post* route on Thursday mornings is enough.

ARTHUR. Aw, Ma.

MA. No, sir. No son of mine is going to get up at four-thirty and miss the sleep God meant him to have.

ARTHUR. *(Sullenly)* Hhm! Ma's always talking about God. I guess she got a letter from him this morning.

(MA rises, outraged)

MA. Elmer, stop that automobile this minute. I don't go another step with anybody that says things like that. Arthur, you get out of this car. *(PA stops the car.)* Elmer, you give him a dollar bill. He can go back to Newark, by himself. I don't want him.

ARTHUR. What did I say? There wasn't anything terrible about that.

ELMER. I didn't hear what he said, Kate.

MA. God has done a lot of things for me and I won't have Him made fun of by anybody. Get out of the car this minute.

CAROLINE. Aw, Ma—don't spoil the ride.

MA. No.

ELMER. We might as well go on, Kate, since we've got started. I'll talk to the boy tonight.

MA. *(Slowly conceding)* All right, if you say so, Elmer. *(PA starts the car.)* But I won't sit beside him. Caroline, you come, and sit by me.

ARTHUR. *(Frightened)* Aw, Ma, that wasn't so terrible.

MA. I don't want to talk about it. I hope your father washes your mouth out with soap and water.—Where'd we all be if I started talking about God like that, I'd like to know! We'd be in the speakeasies and nightclubs and places like that, that's where we'd be.—All right, Elmer, you can go on now.

CAROLINE. *(After a slight pause)* What did he say, Ma? I didn't hear what he said.

MA. I don't want to talk about it.

(They drive on in silence for a moment, the shocked silence after a scandal)

ELMER. I'm going to stop and give the car a little water, I guess.

MA. All right, Elmer. You know best.

ELMER. *(Turns the wheel and stops; to a garage hand)* Could I have a little water in the radiator—to make sure?

THE STAGE MANAGER. *(In this scene alone he lays aside his script and enters into a role seriously)* You sure can. *(He punches the tires)* Air, all right? Do you need any oil or gas?

ELMER. No, I think not. I just got fixed up in Newark.

MA. We're on the right road for Camden, are we?

THE STAGE MANAGER. Yes, keep straight ahead. You can't miss it. You'll be in Trenton in a few minutes.

(He carefully pours some water into the hood)

Camden's a great town, lady, believe me.

MA. My daughter likes it fine—my married daughter.

THE STAGE MANAGER. Yea? It's a great burg all right. I guess I think so because I was born near there.

MA. Well, well. Your folks still live there?

THE STAGE MANAGER. *(Standing with one foot on the rung of* MA'S *chair. They have taken a great fancy to one another.)* No, my old man sold the farm and they built a factory on it. So the folks moved to Philadelphia.

MA. My married daughter Beulah lives there because her husband works in the telephone company.—Stop pokin' me, Caroline!—We're all going down to see her for a few days.

THE STAGE MANAGER. Yea?

MA. She's been sick, you see, and I just felt I had to go and see her. My husband and my boy are going to stay at the Y.M.C.A. I hear they've got a dormitory on the top floor that's real clean and comfortable. Had you ever been there?

THE STAGE MANAGER. No. I'm Knights of Columbus myself.

MA. Oh.

THE STAGE MANAGER. I used to play basketball at the Y though. It looked all right to me.

(He reluctantly shakes himself out of it and pretends to examine the car again, whistling)

Well, I guess you're all set now, lady. I hope you have a good trip; you can't miss it.

EVERYBODY. Thanks. Thanks a lot. Good luck to you.

(The car jolts and lurches)

MA. *(With a sigh)* The world's full of nice people.—That's what I call a nice young man.

CAROLINE. *(Earnestly)* Ma, you oughtn't to tell 'em all everything about yourself.

MA. Well, Caroline, you do your way and I'll do mine.—He looked kinda pale to me. I'd like to feed him up for a few days. His mother lives in Philadelphia and I expect he eats at those dreadful Greek places.

CAROLINE. I'm hungry. Pa, there's a hot dog stand. K'n I have one?

ELMER. We'll all have one, eh, Kate? We had such an early lunch.

MA. Just as you think best, Elmer.

(He stops the car.)

ELMER. Arthur, here's half a dollar. Run over and see what they have. Not too much mustard either.

*(*ARTHUR *descends from the car and goes offstage right.* MA *and* CAROLINE *get out and walk a bit.)*

MA. What's that flower over there? I'll take some of those to Beulah.

CAROLINE. It's just a weed, Ma.

MA. I like it.—My, look at the sky, wouldya! I'm glad I was born in New Jersey. I've always said it was the best state in the Union. Every state has something no other state has got.

(They stroll about humming. Presently ARTHUR *returns with his hands full of imaginary hot dogs which he distributes. He is still very much cast down by the recent scandal. He finally approaches his mother and says falteringly:)*

ARTHUR. Ma, I'm sorry. I'm sorry for what I said.

(He bursts into tears and puts his forehead against her elbow)

MA. There. There. We all say wicked things at times. I know you didn't mean it like it sounded.

(He weeps still more violently than before)

Why, now, now! I forgive you, Arthur, and tonight before you go to bed you . . . *(She whispers)* You're a good boy at heart, Arthur, and we all know it.

*(*CAROLINE *starts to cry too.* MA *is suddenly joyously alive and happy)*

Sakes alive, it's too nice a day for us all to be cryin'. Come now, get in. Caroline, go up in front with your father. Ma wants to sit with her beau.

(CAROLINE sits in front with her father. MA lets ARTHUR get in car ahead of her; then she closes door.)

I never saw such children. Your hot dogs are all getting wet. Now chew them fine, everybody.—All right, Elmer, forward march.

(Car starts. CAROLINE spits.)

—Caroline, whatever are you doing?

CAROLINE. I'm spitting out the leather, Ma.

MA. Then say *Excuse me.*

CAROLINE. Excuse me, please. *(She spits again.)*

MA. What's this place? Arthur, did you see the post office?

ARTHUR. It said Lawrenceville.

MA. Hnn. School kinda. Nice. I wonder what that big yellow house set back was.—Now it's beginning to be Trenton.

CAROLINE. Papa, it was near here that George Washington crossed the Delaware. It was near Trenton, Mama. He was first in war and first in peace and first in the hearts of his countrymen.

MA. *(Surveying the passing world, serene and didactic)* Well, the thing I like about him best was that he never told a lie.

(The children are duly cast down. There is a pause)

There's a sunset for you. There's nothing like a good sunset.

ARTHUR. There's an Ohio license in front of us. Ma, have you ever been to Ohio?

MA. No.

(A dreamy silence descends upon them. CAROLINE *sits closer to her father.* MA *puts her arm around* ARTHUR, *unsentimentally.)*

ARTHUR. Ma, what a lotta people there are in the world, Ma. There must be thousands and thousands in the United States. Ma, how many are there?

MA. I don't know. Ask your father.

ARTHUR. Pa, how many are there?

ELMER. There are a hundred and twenty-six million, Kate.

MA. *(Giving a pressure about* ARTHUR*'s shoulder)* And they all like to drive out in the evening with their children beside 'em.

(Another pause)

Why doesn't somebody sing something? Arthur, you're always singing something; what's the matter with you?

ARTHUR. All right. What'll we sing? *(He sketches:)*

In the Blue Ridge mountains of Virginia,
On the trail of the lonesome pine . . .

No, I don't like that anymore. Let's do:

I been workin' on de railroad

(CAROLINE *joins in.)*

All de liblong day.

(MA *sings.)*

I been workin' on de railroad

(PA *joins in.)*

Just to pass de time away.

(MA *suddenly jumps up with a wild cry.)*

MA. Elmer, that signpost said Camden, I saw it.

ELMER. All right, Kate, if you're sure.

(Much shifting of gears, backing, and jolting)

MA. Yes, there it is. Camden—five miles. Dear old Beulah. *(The journey continues.)*—Now, children, you be good and quiet during dinner. She's just got out of bed after a big sorta operation, and we must all move around kinda quiet. First you drop me and Caroline at the door and just say hello, and then you menfolk go over to the Y.M.C.A. and come back for dinner in about an hour.

CAROLINE. *(Shutting her eyes and pressing her fists passionately against her nose)* I see the first star. Everybody make a wish.
Star light, star bright,
First star I seen tonight.
I wish I may, I wish I might
Have the wish I wish tonight.
(Then solemnly) Pins. Mama, you say "needles."

(She interlocks little fingers with her mother)

MA. Needles.

CAROLINE. Shakespeare. Ma, you say "Longfellow."

MA. Longfellow.

CAROLINE. Now it's a secret and I can't tell it to anybody. Ma, you make a wish.

MA. *(With almost grim humor)* No, I can make wishes without waiting for no star. And I can tell my wishes right out loud too. Do you want to hear them?

CAROLINE. *(Resignedly)* No, Ma, we know 'em already. We've heard 'em.

(She hangs her head affectedly on her mother's left shoulder and says with unmalicious mimicry)

You want me to be a good girl and you want Arthur to be honest in word and deed.

MA. *(Majestically)* Yes. So mind yourself.

ELMER. Caroline, take out that letter from Beulah in my coat pocket by you and read aloud the places I marked with red pencil.

CAROLINE. *(Working)* "A few blocks after you pass the two big oil tanks on your left . . ."

EVERYBODY. *(Pointing backward)* There they are!

CAROLINE. ". . . you come to a corner where there's an A & P store on the left and a firehouse kitty-corner to it . . ."

(They all jubilantly identify these landmarks)

". . . turn right, go two blocks, and our house is Weyerhauser Street Number 471."

MA. It's an even nicer street than they used to live in. And right handy to an A & P.

CAROLINE. *(Whispering)* Ma, it's better than our street. It's richer than our street.—Ma, isn't Beulah richer than we are?

MA. *(Looking at her with a firm and glassy eye)* Mind yourself, missy. I don't want to hear anybody talking about rich or not rich when I'm around. If people aren't nice I don't care how rich they are. I live in the best street in the world because my husband and children live there.

(She glares impressively at CAROLINE *a moment to let this lesson sink in, then looks up, sees* BEULAH *and waves)*

There's Beulah standing on the steps lookin' for us.

*(*BEULAH *has appeared and is waving. They all call out "Hello, Beulah—Hello." Presently they are all getting out of the car)*

BEULAH. Hello, Mama.—Well, lookit how Arthur and Caroline are growing!

MA. They're bursting all their clothes!

BEULAH. *(Kisses her father long and affectionately)* Hello, Papa. Good old Papa. You look tired, Pa—

MA. —Yes, your pa needs a rest. Thank Heaven, his vacation has come just now. We'll feed him up and let him sleep late. Pa has a present for you, Loolie. He would go and buy it.

BEULAH. Why, Pa, you're terrible to go and buy anything for me. Isn't he terrible?

MA. Well, it's a secret. You can open it at dinner.

BEULAH. *(Puts her arm around his neck and rubs her nose against his temple)* Crazy old Pa, goin' buyin' things! It's me that ought to be buyin' things for you, Pa.

ELMER. Oh, no! There's only one Loolie in the world.

BEULAH. *(Whispering, as her eyes fill with tears)* Are you glad I'm still alive, Pa?

(She kisses him abruptly and goes back to the house steps)

ELMER. Where's Horace, Loolie?

BEULAH. He was kep' over a little at the office. He'll be here any minute. He's crazy to see you all.

MA. All right. You men go over to the Y and come back in about an hour.

BEULAH. *(As her father returns to the wheel, she stands out in the street beside him)* Go straight along, Pa, you can't miss it. It just stares at ya.

*(*THE STAGE MANAGER *removes the automobile with the help of* ELMER *and* ARTHUR, *who go off waving their good-byes)*

Well, come on upstairs, Ma, and take off your things. Caroline, there's a surprise for you in the backyard.

CAROLINE. Rabbits?
BEULAH. No.
CAROLINE. Chickens?
BEULAH. No. Go and see.

*(*CAROLINE *runs offstage.* BEULAH *and* MA *gradually go upstairs)*

There are two new puppies. You be thinking over whether you can keep one in Newark.

MA. I guess we can. *(*THE STAGE MANAGER *pushes out a bed from the left. Its foot is toward the right.)* It's a nice house, Beulah. You just got a lovely home.

BEULAH. When I got back from the hospital, Horace had moved everything into it, and there wasn't anything for me to do.

MA. It's lovely.

*(*BEULAH *sits on bed, testing the springs)*

BEULAH. I think you'll find this comfortable, Ma.

MA. *(Taking off her hat)* Oh, I could sleep on a heapa shoes, Loolie! I don't have no trouble sleepin'.

(She sits down beside her)

Now let me look at my girl. Well, well, when I last saw you, you didn't know me. You kep' saying: "When's Mama comin'? When's Mama comin'?" But the doctor sent me away.

BEULAH. *(Puts her head on her mother's shoulder and weeps)*: It was awful, Mama. It was awful. She didn't even live a few minutes, Mama. It was awful.

MA. *(Looking far away)* God thought best, dear. God thought best. We don't understand why. We just go on, honey, doin' our business.

(Then almost abruptly—passing the back of her hand across her cheek)

Well, now, what are we giving the men to eat tonight?

BEULAH. There's a chicken in the oven.

MA. What time didya put it in?

BEULAH. *(Restraining her)* Aw, Ma, don't go yet. *(Taking her mother's hand and drawing her down beside her.)* I like to sit here with you this way. You always get the fidgets when we try and pet ya, Mama.

MA. *(Ruefully, laughing)* Yes, it's kinda foolish. I'm just an old Newark bag-a-bones.

(She glances at the backs of her hands)

BEULAH. *(Indignantly)* Why, Ma, you're good-lookin'! We always said you were good-lookin'.—And besides, you're the best ma we could ever have.

MA. *(Uncomfortable)* Well, I hope you like me. There's nothin' like being liked by your family. *(Rises.)*—Now I'm going downstairs to look at the chicken. You stretch out here for a minute and shut your eyes.—Have you got everything laid in for breakfast before the shops close?

BEULAH. Oh, you know! Ham and eggs.

(They both laugh. MA *puts an imaginary blanket over* BEULAH.*)*

MA. I declare I never could understand what men see in ham and eggs. I think they're horrible.—What time did you put the chicken in?

BEULAH. Five o'clock.

MA. Well, now, you shut your eyes for ten minutes.

*(*BEULAH *stretches out and shuts her eyes.* MA *descends the stairs absentmindedly singing.)*

"There were ninety and nine that safely lay
In the shelter of the fold,
But one was out on the hills away,
Far off from the gates of gold . . ."

End of Play

Pullman Car Hiawatha

Characters

	THE STAGE MANAGER
Compartment Three:	AN INSANE WOMAN, *Mrs. Churchill*
	MALE ATTENDANT, *Mr. Morgan*
	THE FEMALE ATTENDANT, *A trained nurse*
Compartment Two:	PHILIP MILBURY
Compartment One:	HARRIET MILBURY, *Philip's young wife*
Lower One:	A MAIDEN LADY
Lower Three:	A MIDDLE-AGED DOCTOR
Lower Five:	A STOUT, AMIABLE WOMAN
Lower Seven:	AN ENGINEER, *Bill, going to California*
Lower Nine:	AN ENGINEER, *Fred*
	THE PORTER, *Harrison*
	GROVER'S CORNERS, OHIO, *represented by a Grinning Boy*
	THE FIELD, *represented by Somebody in Shirt Sleeves*
	A TRAMP
	PARKERSBURG, OHIO, *represented by a Farmer's Wife and Three Young People*
	A WORKMAN, *Mr. Krüger, a ghost*
	THE WORKER, *a watchman*
	THE WEATHER, *represented by a Mechanic*

The Hours:	TEN O'CLOCK ELEVEN O'CLOCK TWELVE O'CLOCK	*represented by Three Beautiful Women*
The Planets:	SATURN	
	VENUS	
	JUPITER	
	EARTH	
The Archangels:	GABRIEL	
	MICHAEL	

Setting

A Pullman car making its way from New York to Chicago, December 1930.

(At the back of the stage is a balcony or bridge or runway leading out of sight in both directions. Two flights of stairs descend from it to the stage. There is no further scenery.)

(At the rise of the curtain THE STAGE MANAGER *is making lines with a piece of chalk on the floor of the stage by the footlights.)*

THE STAGE MANAGER. This is the plan of a Pullman car. Its name is *Hiawatha* and on December twenty-first it is on its way from New York to Chicago. Here at your left are three compartments. Here is the aisle and five lowers. The berths are all full, uppers and lowers, but for the purposes of this play we are limiting our interest to the people in the lower berths on the further side only. The berths are already made-up. It is half past nine.

Most of the passengers are in bed behind the green curtains. They are dropping their shoes on the floor, or wrestling with their trousers, or wondering whether they dare hide their valuables in the pillow slips during the night. All right! Come on, everybody!

(The actors enter carrying chairs. Each improvises his berth by placing two chairs "facing one another" in his chalk-marked space. They then sit in one chair, profile to the audience, and rest their feet on the other. This must do for lying in bed. The passengers in the compartments do the same. Reading from Left to Right we have: Compartment Three. Compartment Two, Compartment One, Lower One, Lower Three, Lower Five, Lower Seven, Lower Nine.)

LOWER ONE. Porter, be sure and wake me up at quarter of six.

THE PORTER. Yes, ma'am.

LOWER ONE. I know I shan't sleep a wink, but I want to be told when it's quarter of six.

THE PORTER. Yes, ma'am.

LOWER SEVEN. *(Putting his head through the curtains)* Hsst! Porter! Hsst! How the hell do you turn on this other light?

THE PORTER. *(Fussing with it)* I'm afraid it's outta order, suh. You'll have to use the other end.

THE STAGE manager. *(Falsetto, substituting for some woman in an upper berth)* May I ask if someone in this car will be kind enough to lend me some aspirin?

THE PORTER. *(Rushing about)* Yes, ma'am.

LOWER NINE. *(One of the engineers, descending the aisle and falling into Lower Five)* Sorry, lady, sorry. Made a mistake.

LOWER FIVE. *(Grumbling)* Never in all my born days!

LOWER ONE. *(In a shrill whisper)* Porter! Porter!

THE PORTER. Yes, ma'am.

LOWER ONE. My hot water bag's leaking. I guess you'll have to take it away. I'll have to do without it tonight. How awful!

LOWER FIVE. *(Sharply to the passenger above her)* Young man, you mind your own business, or I'll report you to the conductor.

THE STAGE MANAGER. *(Substituting for Upper Five)* Sorry, ma'am, I didn't mean to upset you. My suspenders fell down and I was trying to catch them.

LOWER FIVE. Well, here they are. Now go to sleep. Everybody seems to be rushing into my berth tonight. *(She puts her head out)* Porter! Porter! Be a good soul and bring me a glass of water, will you? I'm parched.

LOWER NINE. Bill!

(No answer)

Bill!

LOWER SEVEN. Yea? Wha'd'ya want?

LOWER NINE. Slip me one of those magazines, willya?

LOWER SEVEN. Which one d'ya want?

LOWER NINE. Either one. *Detective Stories.* Either one.

LOWER SEVEN. Aw, Fred. I'm just in the middle of one of 'em in *Detective Stories.*

LOWER NINE. That's all right. I'll take the *Western.*—Thanks.

THE STAGE MANAGER. *(To the actors)* All right!—Sh! Sh! Sh! *(To the audience)* Now I want you to hear them thinking.

(There is a pause and then they all begin a murmuring-swishing noise, very soft. In turn each one of them can be heard above the others)

LOWER FIVE. *(The Woman of Fifty)* Let's see I've got the doll for the baby. And the slip-on for Marietta. And the fountain pen for Herbert. And the subscription to *Time* for George . . .

LOWER SEVEN. *(Bill)* God! Lillian, if you don't turn out to be what I think you are, I don't know what I'll do.—I guess it's bad politics to let a woman know that you're going all the way to California to see her. I'll think up a song-and-dance about a business trip or something. Was I ever as hot and bothered about anyone like this before? Well, there was Martha. But that was different. I'd better try and read or I'll go cuckoo. "How did you know it was ten o'clock when the visitor left the house?" asked the detective. "Because at ten o'clock," answered the girl, "I always turn out the lights in the conservatory and in the back hall. As I was coming down the stairs I heard the master talking to someone at the front door. I heard him say, 'Well, good night . . .' "—Gee, I don't feel like reading; I'll just think about Lillian. That yellow hair. Them eyes! . . .

LOWER THREE. *(The Doctor reads aloud to himself the most hair-raising material from a medical journal, every now and then punctuating his reading with an interrogative "So?")*

LOWER ONE. *(The Maiden Lady)* I know I'll be awake all night. I might just as well make up my mind to it now. I can't imagine what got hold of that hot water bag to leak on the train of all places. Well now, I'll lie on my right side and breathe deeply and think of beautiful things, and perhaps I can doze off a bit.

(And lastly:)

LOWER NINE. *(Fred)* That was the craziest thing I ever did. It's set me back three whole years. I could have saved up thirty thousand dollars by now, if I'd only stayed over here. What business had I got to fool with contracts with the goddam Soviets. Hell, I thought it would be interesting. Interesting, what the hell! It's set me back three whole years. I don't even know if the company'll take me back. I'm green, that's all. I just don't grow up.

*(*THE STAGE MANAGER *strides toward them with lifted hand, crying, "Hush," and their whispering ceases)*

THE STAGE MANAGER. That'll do!—Just one minute. Porter!

THE PORTER. *(Appearing at the left)* Yessuh.

THE STAGE MANAGER. It's your turn to think. *(*THE PORTER *is very embarrassed)* Don't you want to? You have a right to.

THE PORTER. *(Torn between the desire to release his thoughts and his shyness)* Ah . . . ah . . . I'm only thinkin' about my home in Chicago and . . . and my life insurance.

THE STAGE MANAGER. That's right.

THE PORTER. . . . Well, thank you . . . Thank you.

*(*THE PORTER *slips away, blushing violently, in an agony of self-consciousness and pleasure)*

THE STAGE MANAGER. *(To the audience)* He's a good fellow, Harrison is. Just shy.

(To the actors again) Now the compartments, please.

(The berths fall into shadow. PHILIP *is standing at the door connecting his compartment with his wife's)*

PHILIP. Are you all right, angel?

HARRIET. Yes. I don't know what was the matter with me during dinner.

PHILIP. Shall I close the door?

HARRIET. Do see whether you can't put a chair against it that will hold it half open without banging.

PHILIP. There.—Good night, angel. If you can't sleep, call me and we'll sit up and play Russian Bank.

HARRIET. You're thinking of that awful time when we sat up every night for a week . . . But at least I know I shall sleep tonight. The noise of the wheels has become sort of nice and homely. What state are we in?

PHILIP. We're tearing through Ohio. We'll be in Indiana soon.

HARRIET. I know those little towns full of horse blocks.

PHILIP. Well, we'll reach Chicago very early. I'll call you. Sleep tight.

HARRIET. Sleep tight, darling.

(PHILIP *returns to his own compartment. In Compartment Three, the* MALE ATTENDANT *tips his chair back against the wall and smokes a cigar. The* TRAINED NURSE *knits a stocking. The* INSANE WOMAN *leans her forehead against the windowpane, that is, stares into the audience.)*

THE INSANE WOMAN. *(Her words have a dragging, complaining sound, but lack any conviction)* Don't take me there. Don't take me there.

THE FEMALE ATTENDANT. Wouldn't you like to lie down, dearie?

THE INSANE WOMAN. I want to get off the train. I want to go back to New York.

THE FEMALE ATTENDANT. Wouldn't you like me to brush your hair again? It's such a nice feeling.

THE INSANE WOMAN. *(Going to the door)* I want to get off the train. I want to open the door.

THE FEMALE ATTENDANT. *(Taking one of her hands)* Such a noise! You'll wake up all the nice people. Come and I'll tell you a story about the place we're going to.

THE INSANE WOMAN. I don't want to go to that place.

THE FEMALE ATTENDANT. Oh, it's lovely! There are lawns and gardens everywhere. I never saw such a lovely place. Just lovely.

THE INSANE WOMAN. *(Lies down on the bed)* Are there roses?

THE FEMALE ATTENDANT. Roses! Red, yellow, white . . . just everywhere.

THE MALE ATTENDANT. *(After a pause)* That musta been Cleveland.

THE FEMALE ATTENDANT. I had a case in Cleveland once. Diabetes.

THE MALE ATTENDANT. *(After another pause)* I wisht I had a radio here. Radios are good for *them*. I had a patient once that had to have the radio going every minute.

THE FEMALE ATTENDANT. Radios are lovely. My married niece has one. It's always going. It's wonderful.

THE INSANE WOMAN. *(Half rising)* I'm not beautiful. I'm not beautiful as she was.

THE FEMALE ATTENDANT. Oh, I think you're beautiful! Beautiful.—Mr. Morgan, don't you think Mrs. Churchill is beautiful?

THE MALE ATTENDANT. Oh, fine lookin'! Regular movie star, Mrs. Churchill.

(THE INSANE WOMAN *looks inquiringly at them and subsides.* HARRIET *groans slightly. Smothers a cough. She gropes about with her hand and finds the bell.* THE PORTER *knocks at her door)*

HARRIET. *(Whispering)* Come in. First, please close the door into my husband's room. Softly. Softly.

THE PORTER. *(A plaintive porter)* Yes, ma'am.

HARRIET. Porter, I'm not well. I'm sick. I must see a doctor.

THE PORTER. Why ma'am, they ain't no doctor . . .

HARRIET. Yes, when I was coming out from dinner I saw a man in one of the seats on that side, reading medical papers. Go and wake him up.

THE PORTER. *(Flabbergasted)* Ma'am, I cain't wake anybody up.

HARRIET. Yes, you can. Porter. Porter. Now don't argue with me. I'm very sick. It's my heart. Wake him up. Tell him it's my heart.

THE PORTER. Yes, ma'am.

(He goes into the aisle and starts pulling the shoulder of the man in Lower Three.)

LOWER THREE. Hello. Hello. What is it? Are we there? *(*THE PORTER *mumbles to him)* I'll be right there.—Porter, is it a young woman or an old one?

THE PORTER. I dunno, suh. I guess she's kind a old, suh, but not so very old.

LOWER THREE. Tell her I'll be there in a minute and to lie quietly.

*(*THE PORTER *enters* HARRIET*'s compartment. She has turned her head away.)*

THE PORTER. He'll be here in a minute, ma'am. He says you lie quiet.

*(*LOWER THREE *stumbles along the aisle muttering "Damn these shoes!")*

SOMEONE'S VOICE. Can't we have a little quiet in this car, please?

LOWER NINE. *(Fred)* Oh, shut up!

*(*LOWER THREE *[The Doctor] passes* THE PORTER *and enters* HARRIET*'s compartment. He leans over her, concealing her by his stooping figure)*

LOWER THREE. She's dead, Porter. Is there anyone on the train traveling with her?

THE PORTER. Yessuh. Dat's her husband in dere.

LOWER THREE. Idiot! Why didn't you call him? I'll go in and speak to him.

*(*THE STAGE MANAGER *comes forward)*

THE STAGE MANAGER. All right. So much for the inside of the car. That'll be enough of that for the present. Now for its position geographically, meteorologically, astronomically, theologically considered.

Pullman Car Hiawatha, ten minutes of ten. December twenty-first, 1930. All ready.

(Some figures begin to appear on the balcony.)

No, no. It's not time for The Planets yet. Nor The Hours. *(They retire.)*

*(*THE STAGE MANAGER *claps his hands. A grinning boy in overalls enters from the left behind the berths)*

GROVER'S CORNERS, OHIO. *(In a foolish voice as though he were reciting a piece at a Sunday school entertainment)* I represent Grover's Corners, Ohio. Eight hundred twenty-one souls. "There's so much good in the worst of us and so much bad in the best of us, that it ill behooves any of us to criticize the rest of us." Robert Louis Stevenson. Thankya.

(He grins and goes out right. Enter from the same direction somebody in shirt sleeves. This is a field.)

THE FIELD. I represent a field you are passing between Grover's Corners, Ohio, and Parkersburg, Ohio. In this field there are fifty-one gophers, two hundred and six field mice, six snakes and millions of bugs, insects, ants and spiders. All in their winter sleep. "What is so rare as a day in June? Then, if ever, come perfect days." The Vision of Sir Launfal, William Cullen—I mean James Russell Lowell. Thank you.

(Exit. Enter a tramp)

THE TRAMP. I just want to tell you that I'm a tramp that's been traveling under this car, Hiawatha, so I have a right to be in this play. I'm going from Rochester, New York, to Joliet, Illinois. It takes a lotta people to make a world. "On the road to Mandalay, where the flying fishes play and the sun comes up like thunder, over China, 'cross the bay." Frank W. Service. It's bitter cold. Thank you.

(Exit. Enter a gentle old farmer's wife with three stringy young people)

PARKERSBURG, OHIO. I represent Parkersburg, Ohio. Twenty-six hundred and four souls. I have seen all the dreadful havoc that alcohol has done and I hope no one here will ever touch a drop of the curse of this beautiful country.

(She beats a measure and they all sing unsteadily:)

"Throw out the lifeline! Throw out the lifeline! Someone is sinking today-ay . . ."

*(*THE STAGE MANAGER *waves them away tactfully. Enter a workman)*

THE WORKMAN. Ich bin der Arbeiter der hier sein Leben verlor. Bei der Sprengung für diese Brücke über die Sie in dem Moment fahren—*(The engine whistles for a trestle crossing)*—erschlug mich ein Felsblock. Ich spiele jetzt als Geist in diesem Stück mit. "Vor sieben und achtzig Jahren haben unsere Väter auf diesem Kontinent eine neue Nation hervorgebracht . . ."

THE STAGE MANAGER. *(Helpfully, to the audience)* I'm sorry; that's in German. He says that he's the ghost of a workman who was killed while they were building the trestle over which the car Hiawatha is now passing *(The engine whistles again)*—and he wants to appear in this play. A chunk of rock hit him while they were dynamiting.—His motto you know "Three score and seven years ago our fathers brought forth upon this continent a new nation dedicated . . ." and so on. Thank you, Mr. Krüger.

(Exit the ghost. Enter another worker.)

THE WORKER. I'm a watchman in a tower near Parkersburg, Ohio. I just want to tell you that I'm not asleep and that the signals are all right for this train. I hope you all have a fine trip. "If you can keep your head when all about you are losing theirs and blaming it on you . . ." Rudyard Kipling. Thank you.

(He exits. THE STAGE MANAGER *comes forward)*

THE STAGE MANAGER. All right. That'll be enough of that. Now the weather.

(Enter a MECHANIC.*)*

A MECHANIC. It is eleven degrees above zero. The wind is north-northwest, velocity fifty-seven. There is a field of low barometric pressure moving eastward from Saskatchewan to the eastern coast. Tomorrow it will be cold with some snow in the middle western states and northern New York.

(He exits)

THE STAGE MANAGER. All right. Now for The Hours. *(Helpfully to the audience)* The minutes are gossips; the hours are philosophers; the years are theologians. The hours are philosophers with the exception of Twelve O'clock who is also a theologian.—Ready Ten O'clock!

*(*THE HOURS *are beautiful girls dressed like Elihu Vedder's Pleiades. Each carries a great gold Roman numeral. They pass slowly across the balcony at the back, moving from right to left.)*

What are you doing, Ten O'clock? Aristotle?

TEN O'CLOCK. No, Plato, Mr. Washburn.

THE STAGE MANAGER. Good.—"Are you not rather convinced that he who thus . . ."

TEN O'CLOCK. "Are you not rather convinced that he who thus sees Beauty as only it can be seen will be specially favored? And since he is in contact not with images but with realities . . ." *(She continues the passage in a murmur as* ELEVEN O'CLOCK *appears.)*

ELEVEN O'CLOCK. "What else can I, Epictetus, do, a lame old man, but sing hymns to God? If then I were a nightingale, I would do the nightingale's part. If I were a swan, I would do a swan's. But now I am a rational creature . . ." *(Her voice also subsides to a murmur.* TWELVE O'CLOCK *appears.)*

THE STAGE MANAGER. Good.—Twelve O'clock, what have you?

TWELVE O'CLOCK. Saint Augustine and his mother.

THE STAGE MANAGER. So.—"And we began to say: If to any the tumult of the flesh were hushed . . ."

TWELVE O'CLOCK. "And we began to say: If to any the tumult of the flesh were hushed; hushed the images of earth; of waters and of air . . ."

THE STAGE MANAGER. Faster.—"Hushed also the poles of Heaven."

TWELVE O'CLOCK. "Yea, were the very soul to be hushed to herself."

THE STAGE MANAGER. A little louder, Miss Foster.

TWELVE O'CLOCK. *(A little louder)* "Hushed all dreams and imaginary revelations . . ."

THE STAGE MANAGER. *(Waving them back)* All right. All right. Now The Planets. December twenty-first, 1930, please.

(THE HOURS *unwind and return to their dressing rooms at the right.* THE PLANETS *appear on the balcony. Some of them take their place halfway on the steps. These have no words, but each has a sound. One has a pulsating, zinging sound. Another has a thrum. One whistles ascending and descending scales. Saturn does a slow, obstinate humming sound on two repeated low notes)*

Louder, Saturn.—Venus, higher. Good. Now, Jupiter.—Now the Earth.

(THE STAGE MANAGER *turns to the beds on the train)*

Come, everybody. This is the Earth's sound.

(The towns, workmen, etc., appear at the edge of the stage. The passengers begin their "thinking" murmur.)

Come, Grover's Corners. Parkersburg. You're in this. Watchman. Tramp. This is the Earth's sound.

(He conducts it as the director of an orchestra would. Each of the towns and workmen does his motto. THE INSANE WOMAN *breaks into passionate weeping. She rises and stretches out her arms to* THE STAGE MANAGER.*)*

THE INSANE WOMAN. Use me. Give me something to do.

(He goes to her quickly, whispers something in her ear, and leads her back to her guardians. She is unconsoled.)

THE STAGE MANAGER. Now shh-shh-shh! Enter The Archangels.

(To the audience) We have now reached the theological position of Pullman Car Hiawatha.

(The towns and workmen have disappeared. The Planets, offstage, continue a faint music. Two young men in blue serge suits enter along the balcony and descend the stairs at the right. As they pass each bed the passenger talks in his sleep.)

*(*GABRIEL *points out Bill to* MICHAEL *who smiles with raised eyebrows. They pause before Lower Five, and* MICHAEL *makes the sound of assent that can only be rendered "Hn-Hn.")*

(The remarks that the characters make in their sleep are not all intelligible, being lost in the sound of sigh or groan or whisper by which they are conveyed. But we seem to hear:)

LOWER NINE. *(Loud)* Some people are slower than others, that's all.

LOWER SEVEN. *(Bill)* It's no fun, y'know. I'll try.

LOWER FIVE. *(The lady of the Christmas presents, rapidly)* You know best, of course. I'm ready whenever you are. One year's like another.

LOWER ONE. I can teach sewing. I can sew.

(They approach HARRIET*'s compartment.* THE INSANE WOMAN *sits up and speaks to them)*

THE INSANE WOMAN. Me?

*(*THE ARCHANGELS *shake their heads)*

What possible use can there be in my simply waiting?—Well, I'm grateful for anything. I'm grateful for being so much better than I was. The old story, the terrible story, doesn't haunt me as it used to. A great load seems to have been taken off my mind.—But no one understands me any more. At last I understand myself perfectly, but no one else understands a thing I say.—So I must wait?

(The ARCHANGELS *nod, smiling)*

(Resignedly, and with a smile that implies their complicity) Well, you know best. I'll do whatever is best; but everyone is so childish, so absurd. They have no logic. These people are all so mad . . . These people are like children; they have never suffered.

(She returns to her head and sleeps. The ARCHANGELS *stand beside* HARRIET. *The* DOCTOR *has drawn* PHILIP *into the next compartment and is talking to him in earnest whispers.* HARRIET*'s face has been toward the wall; she turns it slightly and speaks toward the ceiling.)*

HARRIET. I wouldn't be happy there. Let me stay dead down here. I belong here. I shall be perfectly happy to roam about my house and be near Philip.—You know I wouldn't be happy there.

*(*GABRIEL *leans over and whispers into her ear. After a short pause she bursts into fierce tears.)*

I'm ashamed to come with you. I haven't done anything. I haven't done anything with my life. Worse than that: I was angry and sullen. I never realized anything. I don't dare go a step in such a place.

(They whisper to her again.)

But it's not possible to forgive such things. I don't want to be forgiven so easily. I want to be punished for it all. I won't stir until I've been punished a long, long time. I want to be freed of all that—by punishment. I want to be all new.

(They whisper to her. She puts her feet slowly on the ground.)

HARRIET. But no one else could be punished for me. I'm willing to face it all myself. I don't ask anyone to be punished for me.

(They whisper to her again. She sits long and brokenly looking at her shoes, thinking it over.)

It wasn't fair. I'd have been willing to suffer for it myself—if I could have endured such a mountain.

(She smiles) Oh, I'm ashamed! I'm just a stupid and you know it. I'm just another American.—But then what wonderful things must be beginning now. You really want me? You really want me?

(They start leading her down the aisle of the car)

Let's take the whole train. There are some lovely faces on this train. Can't we all come? You'll never find anyone better than Philip. Please, please, let's all go.

(They reach the steps. The ARCHANGELS *interlock their arms as a support for her as she leans heavily on them, taking the steps slowly. Her words are half singing and half babbling.)*

But look at how tremendously high and far it is. I've a weak heart. I'm not supposed to climb stairs. "I do not ask to see the distant scene: One step enough for me." It's like Switzerland. My tongue keeps saying things. I can't control it.—Do let me stop a minute: I want to say good-bye.

(She turns in their arms)

Just a minute, I want to cry on your shoulder.

(She leans her forehead against GABRIEL*'s shoulder and laughs long and softly.)*

Good-bye, Philip.—I begged him not to marry me, but he would. He believed in me just as you do.—Goodbye, 1312 Ridgewood Avenue, Oaksbury, Illinois. I hope I remember all its steps and doors and wallpapers forever. Good-bye, Emerson Grammar School on the corner of Forbush Avenue and Wherry Street. Good-bye, Miss Walker and Miss Cramer who taught me English and Miss Matthewson who taught me biology. Good-bye, First Congregational Church on the corner of Meyerson Avenue and Sixth Street and Dr. McReady and Mrs. McReady and Julia. Good-bye, Papa and Mama . . .

(She turns)

HARRIET. Now I'm tired of saying good-bye.—I never used to talk like this. I was so homely I never used to have the courage to talk. Until Philip came. I see now. I see now. I understand everything now.

(THE STAGE MANAGER *comes forward)*

THE STAGE MANAGER. *(To the actors)* All right. All right.—Now we'll have the whole world together, please. The whole solar system, please.

(The complete cast begins to appear at the edges of the stage. He claps his hands.)

The whole solar system, please. Where's The Tramp?—Where's The Moon?

(He gives two raps on the floor, like the conductor of an orchestra attracting the attention of his forces, and slowly lifts his hand. The human beings murmur their thoughts; The Hours discourse; The Planets chant or hum. HARRIET*'s voice finally rises above them all, saying.)*

HARRIET. "I was not ever thus, nor asked that Thou Shouldst lead me on, and spite of fears, Pride ruled my will: Remember not past years."

(THE STAGE MANAGER *waves them away)*

THE STAGE MANAGER. Very good. Now clear the stage, please. Now we're at Englewood Station, South Chicago. See the university's towers over there! The best of them all.

LOWER ONE. *(The Maiden Lady)* Porter, you promised to wake me up at quarter of six.

THE PORTER. Sorry, ma'am, but it's been an awful night on this car. A lady's been terrible sick.

LOWER ONE. Oh! Is she better?

THE PORTER. No'm. She ain't one jot better.

LOWER FIVE. Young man, take your foot out of my face.

THE STAGE MANAGER. *(Again substituting for Upper Five)* Sorry, lady, I slipped—

LOWER FIVE. *(Grumbling not unamiably)* I declare, this trip's been one long series of insults.

THE STAGE MANAGER. Just one minute, ma'am, and I'll be down and out of your way.

LOWER FIVE. Haven't you got anybody to darn your socks for you? You ought to be ashamed to go about that way.

THE STAGE MANAGER. Sorry, lady.

LOWER FIVE. You're too stuck up to get married. That's the trouble with you.

LOWER NINE. Bill! Bill!

LOWER SEVEN. Yea? Wha'd'ya want?

LOWER NINE. Bill, how much d'ya give the porter on a train like this? I've been outta the country so long . . .

LOWER SEVEN. Hell, Fred, I don't know myself.

THE PORTER. CHICAGO, CHICAGO. All out. This train don't go no further.

(The passengers jostle their way out and an army of old women with mops and pails enter and prepare to clean up the car.)

End of Play

About the Author

In his quiet way, THORNTON NIVEN WILDER was a revolutionary writer who experimented boldly with literary forms and themes, from the beginning to the end of his long career. "Every novel is different from the others," he wrote when he was seventy-five. "The theater (ditto). . . . The thing I'm writing now is again totally unlike anything that preceded it." Wilder's richly diverse settings, characters, and themes are at once specific and global. Deeply immersed in classical as well as contemporary literature, he often fused the traditional and the modern in his novels and plays, all the while exploring the cosmic in the commonplace. In a January 12, 1953, cover story, *Time* took note of Wilder's unique "planetary mind"—his ability to write from a vision that was at once American and universal.

A pivotal figure in the history of twentieth-century letters, Wilder was a novelist and playwright whose works continue to be widely read and produced in this new century. He is the only writer to have won the Pulitzer Prize for both fiction and drama. His second novel, *The Bridge of San Luis Rey,* received the fiction award in 1928, and he won the prize twice in drama, for *Our Town* in 1938 and *The Skin of Our Teeth* in 1943. His other novels are *The Cabala, The Woman of Andros, Heaven's My Destination, The Ides of March, The Eighth Day,* and *Theophilus North.* His other major dramas include *The Matchmaker,* which was adapted as the internationally acclaimed musical comedy *Hello, Dolly!,* and *The Alcestiad.* Among his innovative, frequently performed shorter plays are *The Happy Journey to Trenton and Camden* and *The Long Christmas Dinner* (1931). In the 1950s, he conceived a unique dramatic series, *The Ages of Man* and *The Seven*

Deadly Sins, completing four of the plays he envisioned in each group. Three of the plays were first performed in 1962 as *Plays for Bleecker Street.*

Wilder and his work received many honors, highlighted by the three Pulitzer Prizes, the Gold Medal for Fiction from the American Academy of Arts and Letters, the Order of Merit (Peru), the Goethe-Plakette der Stadt (Germany, 1959), the Presidential Medal of Freedom (1963), the National Book Committee's first National Medal for Literature (1965), and the National Book Award for Fiction (1967).

He was born in Madison, Wisconsin, on April 17, 1897, to Amos Parker Wilder and Isabella Niven Wilder. The family later lived in China and in California, where Wilder was graduated from Berkeley High School. After two years at Oberlin College, he went on to Yale, where he received his undergraduate degree in 1920. A valuable part of his education took place during summers spent working hard on farms in California, Kentucky, Vermont, Connecticut, and Massachusetts. His father arranged these rigorous "shirtsleeve" jobs for Wilder and his older brother, Amos, as part of their initiation into the American experience.

Thornton Wilder studied archaeology and Italian as a special student at the American Academy in Rome (1920–21) and earned a master of arts degree in French literature at Princeton in 1926.

In addition to his talents as playwright and novelist, Wilder was an accomplished teacher, essayist, translator, scholar, lecturer, librettist, and screenwriter. In 1942, he teamed with Alfred Hitchcock to write the first draft of the screenplay for the classic thriller *Shadow of a Doubt,* receiving credit as principal writer and a special screen credit for his "contribution to the preparation" of the production. All but fluent in four languages, Wilder translated and adapted plays by such varied authors as Henrik Ibsen, Jean-Paul Sartre, and André Obey. As a scholar, he conducted significant research on James Joyce's *Finnegans Wake* and the plays of Spanish dramatist Lope de Vega.

Wilder's friends included a broad spectrum of figures on both sides of the Atlantic—Hemingway, Fitzgerald, Alexander Woollcott, Gene Tunney, Sigmund Freud, producer Max Reinhardt, Katharine Cornell, Ruth Gordon, and Garson Kanin. Beginning in the mid-1930s, Wilder was especially close to Gertrude Stein and became one of her most effective interpreters and champions. Many of Wilder's friendships are documented in his prolific correspondence. Wilder believed that great letters constitute a "great branch of literature." In a lecture entitled "On Reading the Great Letter Writers," he wrote that a letter can function as a "literary exercise," the "profile of a personality," and "news of the soul," apt descriptions of thousands of letters he wrote to his own friends and family.

Wilder enjoyed acting and played major roles in several of his own plays in summer theater productions. He also possessed a lifelong love of music; reading musical scores was a hobby, and he wrote librettos for two operas based on his work: *The Long Christmas Dinner*, with composer Paul Hindemith, and *The Alcestiad*, with compuser Louise Talma. Both works premiered in Germany.

Teaching was one of Wilder's deepest passions. He began his teaching career in 1921 as an instructor in French at Lawrenceville, a private secondary school in New Jersey. Financial independence after the publication of *The Bridge of San Luis Rey* permitted him to leave the classroom in 1928, but he returned to teaching in the 1930s at the University of Chicago. For six years, on a part-time basis, he taught courses in comparative literature, classics in translation, and composition. In 1950–51, he served as the Charles Eliot Norton Professor of Poetry at Harvard. Wilder's gifts for scholarship and teaching (he treated the classroom as all but a theater) made him a consummate, much sought-after lecturer in his own country and abroad. After World War II, he held special standing, especially in Germany, as an interpreter of his own country's intellectual traditions and their influence on cultural expression.

During World War I, Wilder had served a three-month stint as an enlisted man in the Coast Artillery section of the army, stationed at Fort Adams, Rhode Island. He volunteered for service in World War II, advancing to the rank of lieutenant colonel in Army Air Force Intelligence. For his service in North Africa and Italy, he was awarded the Legion of Merit, the Bronze Star, the Chevalier Legion d'Honneur, and honorary officership in the Military Order of the British Empire (M.B.E.).

From royalties received from *The Bridge of San Luis Rey*, Wilder built a house for his family in 1930 in Hamden, Connecticut, just outside New Haven. But he typically spent as many as two hundred days a year away from Hamden, traveling to and settling in a variety of places that provided the stimulation and solitude he needed for his work. Sometimes his destination was the Arizona desert, the MacDowell Colony in New Hampshire, Martha's Vineyard, Saratoga Springs, Vienna, or Baden-Baden. He wrote aboard ships, and he often chose to stay in "spas in off-season." He needed a certain refuge when he was deeply immersed in writing a novel or play. Wilder explained his habit to a *New Yorker* journalist in 1959: "The walks, the quiet—all the elegance is present, everything is there but the people. That's it! A spa in off-season! I'll make a practice of it."

But Wilder always returned to "the house *The Bridge* built," as it is still known to this day. He died there of a heart attack on December 7, 1975.

READ MORE BY THORNTON WILDER

THEOPHILUS NORTH
A Novel
"An extremely entertaining array of American life in a bygone era."
—*New Yorker*

THE BRIDGE OF SAN LUIS REY
A Novel
"As close to perfect a moral fable as we are ever likely to get in American literature."
—Russell Banks, foreword to *The Bridge of San Luis Rey*

THE CABALA and THE WOMAN OF ANDROS
Two Novels
"No matter where and when Wilder's novels take place, his characters grapple with universal questions about the nature of human existence."
—Penelope Niven, author of *Thornton Wilder*

THE EIGHTH DAY
A Novel
"We marvel at a novel of such spiritual ambition."
—John Updike, foreword to *The Eighth Day*

HEAVEN'S MY DESTINATION
A Novel
"If John Steinbeck's mighty *The Grapes of Wrath* is the tragic novel of the Great Depression, then *Heaven's My Destination* is its comic masterpiece."
—J. D. McClatchy, foreword to *Heaven's My Destination*

THE IDES OF MARCH
A Novel
"Full of the wisdom of the ages—as well as satirical observations on man's political instability, loves, joys and terrors."
—*Chicago Tribune*

HARPER PERENNIAL

THE SKIN OF OUR TEETH
A Play

"For an American dramatist, all roads lead back to Thornton Wilder."
—Paula Vogel, foreword to *The Skin of Our Teeth*

THE MATCHMAKER
A Farce in Four Acts

"Loud, slap dash and uproarious . . . extraordinarily original and funny."
—*New York Times*

THREE PLAYS
Our Town, The Skin of Our Teeth,* and *The Matchmaker

"These plays are a gift." —John Guare, foreword to *Three Plays*

THORNTON WILDER: A LIFE
by Penelope Niven

"The best kind of literary biography, one likely to send the reader back (or perhaps for the first time) to the author's works." —*Washington Post*

THE SELECTED LETTERS OF THORNTON WILDER

"A remarkable collection. . . . What emerges from these pages is a new and sometimes surprising self-portrait of a great American artist."
—Marian Seldes

HARPER PERENNIAL